Murder on the Mississippi

A Karen Prince Mystery

By

Sandra Principe

ISBN: 0-9767954-0-X (paperback)

Published by: Galena Publishing; PO Box 18; Galena, IL 61036.

Acknowledgements

I would like to thank my family and friends who read the early version of this book for their time and comments, including: Barb Alexander, Vince Amato, Alice Begun, Larry Begun, Pam Boneham, James Drummond, Susan Farber, Sara Jean Gray, Lina Haycraft, Patricia Lehnhardt, Deb Malone Lisa Melnick, Laurie Principe, Ralph and Tissy Principe, Linda Puvogel, Marsha Rinetti, Carol Seelig, Wanda Ryan, and Rosanne Wray. Once again, I thank Daryl Watson, Director of the Galena Historical Society for sharing his knowledge of Galena history with me. I also thank Captain Donald Sawvel for the information on barges operating on the Mississippi River.

Disclaimer

Dedication
To Beegs, with love.

Chapter One

A Celebration

I rolled my chair back from my easel and looked at my nearly completed painting. Glowing white lilies, yellow daffodils, and dense blue hyacinths stood out against the dark background. The glass vase was taking shape. Leaning over the rim of the vase was a pink and white wild orchid. This was Orchis Spectabilis, a/k/a Showy Orchid. The blossoms are an inch long and rise in a cluster of seven blooms from between two glossy green leaves.

My name is Karen Prince and I live in the as yet unspoiled rolling hills of northwestern Illinois, in the countryside outside Galena. And yes, we really have wild orchids. They bloom in May, at the same time the delectable morel mushrooms appear. Morels are a gourmet treat selling for $30 a pound. I wouldn't sell my fabulous fungi, even if I hadn't become wealthy beyond belief last year courtesy of a winning lottery ticket.

I know it seems incredible that I won the lottery. In fact, it still sort of seems that way to me. The fact is 17 people won the Power Ball this past year alone, and there were hundreds of winners in other state lotteries. I just happen to be one of those lucky people. But I digress.

I was telling you about my painting. I spent hours yesterday sketching this orchid in its natural environment. That is to say, on the cold damp ground of a north facing wooded slope, next to an old dying elm, among the strips of fallen bark and emerging mayapples and morels. Much as I'd have liked to move this orchid to my garden, I knew it wouldn't survive the transplanting. And I couldn't bring myself to cut it. So I drew it instead, and now it would live on in my painting, *Spring Glory*.

My studio is long and narrow, with a 16 foot ceiling and a full wall of seven-foot tall north windows. The windows start five feet off the ground. Black blinds rise from the bottom sill, reaching up about two feet, so that light streams into the room from above onto the flowers and my canvas. The flowers I paint usually sit on a wooden table to the right of my easel. This lets me view my set-up with light falling on it from the upper left which is the same illumination scheme that was used by the eighteenth century Dutch floral painters whose work I study. Jean-Pierre Rampal's flute music floated from my stereo system.

My brushes were laid out to my left like surgical tools, grouped by type of bristle and size. My palette was to my right, its fresh paints duly mixed with my own Maroger painting medium, and placed in the same position on the palette each morning. Keeping these tools in the same location frees me from consciously thinking about them during the painting process, so that I remain immersed in that wondrous creative other-world while working.

I scooted myself back to the easel and my hand moved in harmony with the music. The tip of my No. 6 bristle brush gently mixed cadmium yellow deep with black to form a rich shadowy green. I laid in the shadow form of a yellow daffodil. Then, with a No. 4 bristle brush, I picked up just enough brilliant cadmium yellow light to create the first petal. Following the form of the petal with my eye, the image moved through my hand, varying the pressure of the brush so that the yellow veining of the petal, with each of its twists and turns, appeared on the canvas in a single stroke. Petal by petal the creation was taking form. I focused on each bend in each petal as closely as an ant walking up and down the hills and valleys of the petals. I was jarred from this meditative state by the decidedly unharmonious ring of the phone.

I glanced at my watch as I reached for the phone on the counter next to me. Two-thirty! Darn! I had to be at the dock by four, a good 45 minutes away. That left me less than an hour to clean my brushes, my palette, and myself!

"Hello," I held the receiver to my ear with one hand while gathering my brushes with the other.

"Karen, I wasn't sure if you'd still be there. Glad I caught you." I could barely hear Mark through the crackly static of his cell phone.

"Yes, I'm still here. Just a minute—there, I've got the headset on now. Where are you?" As I spoke I wiped the paint from my brushes and dipped them in solvent.

"Just past Freeport. The traffic's been ridiculous for a Sunday morning!" Late again, I thought, but said, "Well, you'd better head straight to the boat. No point in coming here now. I hope you make it before we leave the dock!"

"Sorry, Karen. But I'll be there," Mark said, with more confidence than I thought reasonable given the circumstances. Mark was my friend, boyfriend I guess you'd say, though neither of us were kids. I'm 46, and Mark's a few years behind me. We have this comfortable long distance relationship—well, used to be comfortable. And it mostly still is—when we're together. The problem is getting us together. Mark is not a country sort of guy while I definitely have my roots sunk into this Jo Daviess county soil.

"You know where you're going?" I asked. "It's Frentress Lake Marina. Just stay on Highway 20 past Galena. You'll come to a fork in the road where 84 splits off to the right. Don't take 84. Stay on 20. You'll be on divided highway. It's all farm land, except you'll pass a quarry on your right. The marina's on your left. Follow the signs for the old Silver Eagle gambling boat. We're on the *Mississippi Lady*. We leave the dock at five."

"See...crackle crackle..."

"Mark? Can you hear me?"

Crackle, crackle. Dial tone. I hung up and the phone rang again.

"Karen, I'll see you at the boat. We're breaking up."

We seem to be, I thought, but said, "See you there."

This afternoon we were celebrating the first Turning Points Foundation Grant. The purpose of the Grant is to help individuals who want to make a midlife career change into the arts. I'd set up Turning Points last July with a portion of the windfall that came to me as the beneficiary of a randomly generated Power Ball ticket and an astonishing stroke of luck. Stranger things have happened, I suppose, but not to me. Interestingly, winning the lottery had not changed my life as much as the decision I'd made a few years earlier, to leave my law practice and paint full time. The best step I'd made had been to follow my dreams, and I wanted to use this gift to help other people do the same thing. Polly Andrews, my friend and the best PR person in Chicago, organized the Board of Directors and got the Foundation off the ground.

The winner of the first Turning Points Foundation Grant was a woman named Bella Donna. She would receive a five-year living expense grant to start her on her way to becoming a master chef. She was just the sort of candidate I'd hoped to find: smart, hard working, with a burning desire to pursue her dream. Bella's vision was to open her own catering business and write a cookbook of her Italian recipes.

During the grant interviews, Bella had met a friend of mine, Rae Fine. Rae is a New York real estate investor, with deep family roots in Dubuque. She'd just purchased The Red House on West Fourth Street and turned it into a special event location. Rae had designed a full chef's kitchen to Bella's specifications and now this would be Bella's workplace and a venue for her wonderful meals. Bella had prepared an

4

Italian feast for tonight's celebratory cruise—a great way to introduce her culinary talents to tonight's guests, a hundred of whom would be arriving shortly!

I rushed through my "end of painting session" tasks: washing the brushes, scraping the palette, and covering my canvas.

Closing the studio door behind me, I whirled down the spiral staircase in the old silo that connected my studio to my bedroom. I jumped in and out of the shower and wiggled into the blue Donna Karan blouse and slacks I'd selected this morning. Checking the fit in the mirror, I cursed the chocolates I'd eaten last night. Oh well! I blow dried my hair and noticed a few more gray strands mixed in with the brown. But hey, the brown was still winning! I applied the shadow and mascara that an Oak Street makeup consultant had insisted I needed "to bring out my blue eyes." I looked in the mirror and, yep, there they were! Ready, set, I grabbed my purse, said good-bye to Truffles, my cat, and dashed out the door.

Blackjack Road was the perfect twisty country road for my little silver Boxster. With the top down, the spring air blew over me, lifting my hair off my shoulders and pushing it straight back. I leaned into the turns and smiled. The trees along the road were a haze of yellow-green. Red Angus cows grazed in the pastures, their young standing on spindly legs next to them. The cornfields' freshly plowed black earth imparted a sense of order and hope, as well as the scent of "natural fertilizer." Spring was in the air!

On the drive to Frentress Lake I ran through my speech. I'd keep it brief—just long enough to thank the Board and introduce Bella. I hoped Mark would make it on time. I also hoped the tension underscoring our phone conversation would dissipate once we were actually together. It'd been three months since I'd been in Chicago. We'd had an incredibly romantic Valentine's Day weekend. Then I'd spent the next four weeks on the Hawaiian island of Kauai. After my return, Mark had promised to come out to Galena several times but, in the end, the country had not enticed him. Nor, apparently, had I. It was this difference in our choice of homes, city versus country, which was becoming a strain in our relationship. Neither of us was clingy, but seeing each other for a few days every few months wasn't ideal either. Something had to give.

Driving by the Galena Art Museum, or the GAM, as we call it, I thought about the new exhibition. I couldn't wait to spend time with the paintings on loan from private collections all around the world. I'd done tons of research on the artists, including American artists Martin Johnson Heade and Severin Roesen, as well as the most famous of the Dutch floral painters from the 1700's, Rachel Ruysch and Jan Van Huysum. The quality of their work was phenomenal—the clarity of the colors, the refinement of the brush strokes, the grace and balance of the compositions. These were truly works of fine art. By my definition, that means they create a feeling of beauty and grace that uplifts the soul of the viewer. I spun thoughts on this theme, preparing for my speech at the GAM next week, and made voice notes on the mini recorder I carried in the car for just this purpose. I do some of my best thinking driving along these winding country roads.

Before I knew it, I was at the marina. I pulled into the parking lot next to an extraordinarily large woman in a crisp white jacket and slacks, with black hair swept up in a twist. She was loading large trays of food into the waiting arms of three young men, each of whom wore similar white outfits.

"Bella!"

"Ciao, Karen!"

"Great day to be on the River!"

"Yes, thank heavens! I worried about spring rain all week!"

"Well, it couldn't be better today!" I said, and pressed the bat mobile button to raise the top on the Boxster.

Bella and I hugged, both beaming with the joy of friendship, new adventures, and the upcoming celebration. I looked into the back of the van and saw more silver trays loaded with Bella's Italian specialties. There were: *asperaragi e fungi primavera* (spring asparagus and mushrooms), *polenta con formaggio* (a wonderful cornmeal cake topped with goat cheese), *polo con herbi* (roasted chicken with rosemary), and *biscotti* (a crunchy twice baked cookie). Bella's entourage returned and she loaded them, and us as well, with the rest of the brimming platters.

The *Mississippi Lady* was an impressive boat. There were three decks, all painted bright white, with black trim outlining the doorways. She was a 50 year old paddle wheeler and spent her days from April to October docked at Frentress Harbor, making daily excursions up and down the Mississippi. The lower deck housed the galley and the dining room, where Bella now led us. I deposited my tray and returned topside, leaving Bella and her crew to arrange the buffet.

The main deck had a wide walkway all around the perimeter. There were a dozen tables and benches affixed to the center of the main deck. At the bow, a narrow platform jutted out over the water. You could access the platform through a hinged gate in the deck railing. It looked way too precarious to me.

Suddenly the deck vibrated. Looking up, I saw the Captain at the controls in the pilot house. A few crew members in black and white uniforms moved about the main deck. They stowed lines, hoisted bumpers, and polished assorted boat paraphernalia in preparation for our three hour cruise on the Mississippi.

Taking the metal stairs back down to the lower level, I found Bella just finishing her work. A long table draped to the floor in white linen held her creations, as well as plates, silverware and a gorgeous bouquet.

"Our guests will be arriving shortly," I said.

"Yes, they will!" Bella beamed, as she pulled her chef's toque from the back of her waist band, popped it into full glory and placed it squarely on her head. The hat added eight inches more to her six foot frame.

Bella straightened her apron and added, "We're ready for them!"

"Let's go up and meet them as they come on board."

We went out the double swinging doors at the stern of the ship and up the flight of stairs to the main deck. Looking over the ship's rail, we watched as our first guests pulled into the lot.

Peter Pierpoint parked his Mercedes and held the door open for his wife, Graziella Della Giardina, and their daughter, Rosa. Rosa was a beautiful young woman with flowing chestnut hair. She had the figure of a goddess but hid it with an exaggerated slouch. Rosa was shy, perhaps uncomfortable speaking English instead of Italian. Peter hovered protectively behind them, as the trio boarded the *Mississippi Lady*. The family had moved to Galena a year ago from Morrovalle, Italy, to allow Peter to return to his home town and head the GAM.

"Ciao, Bella! Cara mia," Graziella called out as she stepped from the gangway onto the main deck. Graziella and Bella had met only a few months ago, but their shared Italian heritage gave them much in common, and they'd become fast friends.

"Ciao, Graziella, Rosa, e Pietro," Bella replied, holding onto the broad band of her chef's hat with one hand and hugging Graziella with the other.

"Congratulations, Bella!" Peter said, then disappeared in the white cloud of Bella's embrace and emerged laughing. Bella's *joie de vivre* was infectious and we chatted excitedly.

Peter and I had become friends when he was the Director of the Museo di Arte in Morrovalle and I was there to see the exhibit, *Floral Paintings of Florence and Amsterdam*. It was then that I'd first met Graziella, and learned of Peter's connections to Galena. He'd been born on a small farm near here 38 years ago. He'd been a child prodigy and his teachers urged his parents to send him to a private boarding school in Chicago. Their church had raised his tuition, and, with a mixture of sadness and pride, his parents had sent him away to school at fourteen. He'd tested out of most of his high school classes and had his college degree by eighteen. In college he had become fascinated by the art of the Renaissance and had done his graduate work in Art History in Florence. By the time we'd met, he had been the Director of the Museo di Arte for five years. It was in Morrovalle that he had met and married Graziella. So, a few years later when the GAM Director retired, I contacted Peter. It was a perfect opportunity for him to reconnect with his roots and use his unique expertise.

Other guests began arriving now. There was Lois Fretmeyer, the GAM curator; Evan Quinn, Peter's intern at the GAM; Evan's father, Dirk Quinn, a trust and estate lawyer who also happened to be the Chairman of GAM's Board; the Turning Points board members and their spouses; and my neighbors and friends. A young man carrying a huge bouquet came up the ramp and asked for Karen Prince. I looked at Bella, but she shook her head and raised her eyebrows indicating she had no idea who'd sent them. The card read: "Sorry we couldn't be there, but thinking of you, Love and congratulations, Alice and Donald." My friend Alice was like a sister to me. We celebrated most of life's major events together, so I missed her tonight. Alice and her boyfriend, Donald, were on a long planned safari. They were probably in a jeep staring at a lioness and her cubs right now, or perhaps watching thousands of zebras dash across the plains, a pack of hyenas in hot pursuit. As I stood there wondering about Alice, one of Bella's helpers appeared and took the flowers down to the salon for me.

Captain George Bellows came down from the pilot house and introduced himself to us. He was a size match for Bella, and wore his captain's uniform and hat on a strong, erect frame. He had the weathered face of an outdoorsman and clear piercing eyes that inspired confidence. He told us he'd recently retired from the Navy and taken this captain's position because he couldn't bear to be parted from piloting. He joined the receiving line just as Polly Andrews came on board.

"Polly! Well, we did it!" I exclaimed, exchanging jubilant smiles. Polly was beautiful, blonde, and in her late thirties. She was one of those people who immediately became the center of attention wherever she went.

"Yes, we did, didn't we! But it's your brain child, Karen, so the credit is really all yours!"

"Not at all! You know what they say: creation is one percent inspiration and 99 percent perspiration!"

"Not in my new outfit!" Polly laughed. She wore a white Armani pant suit, with a graceful line, custom tailored to emphasize her size six figure. I smiled again as Polly moved on to greet Captain Bellows, standing to my right. Next came the Browns.

Dara and Raymond Brown were sponsors of the *Flowers in Art Exhibit* at the GAM. Dara had inherited the Midwest Packing Plant, started by her great grandfather. MPP was now an international concern, and Dara's husband headed the MPP Board of Directors. They could have lived anywhere in the world, but chose to stay close to their roots and generously contributed to local cultural events and charities. GAM held a special place in Dara's heart. It had been started by her mother, 20 years earlier, and Dara supported it as her mother's legacy to the community.

"Karen, how good to see you and celebrate your wonderful new foundation!"

"Thank you, Dara! So glad you could be here! And the GAM Exhibit is stunning! Have you seen it yet?"

"I stopped by on Friday when Lois was hanging it. It'll be nice for Galena to have this," she said.

"Nice is an understatement! This is an incredible opportunity. Most of those paintings are from private collections so this may well be the only chance to see them."

"You're talking at the Opening this week aren't you?" Dara asked.

"Yes. I'm giving the Gallery Talk on Friday."

"I'll look forward to it," Dara said, and moved on to shake hands with the Captain. Raymond Brown stood behind his wife, shook my hand and moved on with Dara.

A steady stream of passengers walked up the gangway and through the receiving line. Within 30 minutes, the *Mississippi Lady* was buzzing with chatter. The guests were ready to spend a pleasant evening eating, drinking, and watching the world go by from the happy confines of the boat. Captain Bellows returned to the pilot house, and Bella excused herself to check on the buffet tables.

Mark still had not arrived, and I was beginning to worry that he might actually miss the boat. I was contemplating asking our Captain to delay our departure a quarter hour when Mark came running up the gangplank. "Just made it!" Mark said, batting his brown eyes at me and giving me a sheepish grin. The ship's horn gave three long warning blasts.

"So you did," I said, a bit put out by his last minute drama. But I let that slip away, as he gave me a hug and kiss. "Peter, Graziella, Rosa, this is Mark Jordan."

"Mark, so good to meet you. I've heard so much about you," Peter said, extending his hand.

As they shook hands a deep voice boomed over the loud speakers, "Ladies and Gentlemen, this is Captain Bellows. Welcome on board the *Mississippi Lady*. We'll be cruising the Mississippi River today, heading north to Lock and Dam Number 11, then south to Lock and Dam Number 12. I'll point out scenes of particular interest to you along the way. So make yourself comfortable for our cruise."

At the end of the announcement there was a rumble from the engines. The deckhands hurried to their positions along the railings. We watched as ropes were pulled in and stored, the gangplank raised, and our ship pulled away from land. Soon the dock faded into the distance. We were on a slough of the Mississippi at this point, heading out to the main channel. Maple trees lined the shore, but they weren't fully leafed out, and I caught glimpses of small houses set behind them. These homes had gorgeous views of the water, but they were also within a few hundred feet of the railroad tracks. You'd have to be a real rail aficionado to live that close to the freight trains that rumbled through there day and night. With the boats, the River, and a casino, it was a little Riviera.

There was something about watching the world go by from a boat. I figured I'd let everyone enjoy the novelty of the cruise and socialize over Bella's delicious dinner for an hour or so, then make my presentation and comments just before the music started around 6:30 p.m..

"Can I get anyone a drink?" Mark offered, looking around our little group.

"Yes, thank you, Mark. But let us all go and look at this feast of Bella's and have a toast to our hostess!" Graziella said in her heavily accented English. Peter stood between his wife and daughter and put his arms around their shoulders, and said, "An excellent idea. And I'll help you with those drinks, Mark."

There were four stairwells leading down to the main salon: two at the stern—port and starboard; and two at the bow—again, port and starboard. We walked single file down the white metal stairs and entered the main salon.

People circled the buffet table, selected food and chatted. We did the same, then returned to the upper deck and sat at a table near the bow. Mark made a gracious toast, and we watched the scenery change as we entered the main channel of the River.

Limestone bluffs rose 200 feet above the shoreline. Several well spaced mansions were perched on top, overlooking the River. If this were Chicago, there would be high-rise condos side by side. But it wasn't. There was space to live and breathe, and see the light filter through the trees. This was the Midwest at its finest.

In the 1800's, the Mississippi had been the main means of transporting goods between the North and South. Half of our forests had probably floated down this very River. Today, barges carried tons of grain raised by Midwest farmers. We passed a flotilla of barges being pushed downstream as we headed up river.

The Captain's voice boomed over the loudspeaker, "We are approaching the Iowa-Wisconsin Bridge, built in 1868. This is a 340 foot long, 600 ton swing span built on concrete piers. Also in 1868, an

865 foot tunnel was carved through sheer rock to this bridge. Many workers lost their lives working on this project.

"To our left, on the Dubuque side of the River, is the limestone Shot Tower. This was built in 1856 and is named because it was a factory for lead shot used by muzzle loading rifles during the Civil War. Molten lead was dropped from the top of the tower into vats of water in the base of the tower. The lead formed into drops as it fell, and then hardened in the water. It was then collected and sorted into various sizes of lead shot.

"This River is 2,430 miles long from Minnesota to New Orleans. 1.24 million square miles of watershed drain into the Mississippi. That is the third largest watershed drainage in the world.

"Ahead is Lock and Dam Number 11. The Lock and Dam System was started in 1930 and finished in 1937. There are 29 lock and dams in the upper Mississippi between Minneapolis, Minnesota and St. Louis, Missouri. This system makes navigation possible through the entire Mississippi River.

"Up there to your right is the Wisconsin-Illinois state line marked on a tree five feet above the waterline. Iowa is to your left. This is the heart of the Tri-State region." A blue heron perched along the bank and flew upstream as we approached. The Captain continued, "The River is nearly a mile wide at this point and gets wider as it travels south. The River is 30 to 35 feet deep here. We're traveling at a speed of six knots or nautical miles per hour upstream, against the current. When we turn around we will be traveling at eight knots, with the current."

"This dam ahead of us is 1,278 feet long. It was named for Lt. Pike who was in this area in 1805. The city of Dubuque, on your left, is named for Julien Dubuque. Julien Dubuque came to this area in 1788, died here in 1810 and is buried at the top of the bluff just south of here. The park to the right of us now is Eagle Point Park. That park is one of the top ten sights in the Midwest due to its spectacular view of the Mississippi River and the Tri-State area.

"The Blackhawk Wars were fought here in 1832. The Indians were forced to leave their land and flee across the Mississippi. There were no bridges then, of course, and many of them lost their lives here.

"In the 1840's, lead mining became a booming industry here and the lead ore was shipped south on this River. The Mesquakie Indians mined lead in this area for decades dating back prior to the Revolutionary War.

"In 1890 there were 60 button factories along the River making buttons from mussel shells. That industry was started in 1884 by J. F. Boepple. It was relatively short lived however, as the mussels were over harvested and the buttons were later made from plastic.

"That barge you see going down river is 195 feet long. One barge carries 1500 tons of cargo. There are 15 barges in a standard tow. That's 22,500 tons of cargo being pushed in that tow there.

"As we cruise down the River you will see the buildings established by the Sisters of Charity. Mary Frances Clarke came from Dublin to Philadelphia with four companions in 1833 to teach the immigrants. She founded the Sisters of Charity of the Blessed Virgin Mary that same year. In 1843, 19 Sisters moved to Dubuque. At that time this land was part of the Iowa Territories and became a State in 1846. In 1843, Mary Frances Clarke established a school for girls on the prairie, one of the first boarding schools for young women west of the Mississippi River. By 1892 when the order built the new Mother House here, there were 1,500 Sisters of Charity. Today there are less than 1,000. To this date, 5,000 nuns have lived and worked in this order. St. Mary's Academy, the school founded by Clarke on the prairie, has become Clarke College, with 1,200 students there today."

Looking up at the bluffs, I said to Graziella, "This is so beautiful. Do you have anything like this in Morrovalle?"

"Ah, no, no river like this. But our land looks very much like your farmlands here."

"Do you miss it? Italy, I mean."

"Yes, I do. I miss it very much. Our farm has been in the family for many, many generations. I grew up there, and it is my heritage to be with my family and our land. My cousin Umberto is running the vineyard while we are here. Yes, I miss it and Rosa here does too. Don't you, Rosa?"

Rosa looked up shyly and smiled. "Yes, I miss my friends and my cousins, too."

"You've made friends here, haven't you?" I asked. Rosa blushed so deeply that I wondered if there was a young man in her life.

"Yes, I have made some friends."

"Actually, Peter and I are thinking to send Rosa back to live with my cousin Umberto, and to go to school in *Fierenze.*"

"Really!" I managed. The last thing I wanted was for Peter to leave the Museum. He'd done a great job and brought such a depth of experience. "And you and Peter would stay here?"

"Yes, of course," Peter answered for her.

A shadow fell on our table. I looked up to see Dirk Quinn. Dirk was a slight man, with thinning hair and black glasses. Peter stood, shook hands with him and introduced him to Mark. Graziella's hello was cool, and Rosa remained silent.

"Dirk, glad you could join us." I don't know why I said that, maybe because I wasn't glad to see him and that was all that filled my mind at the moment. "I hear you're working on extending the exhibition's tour after the GAM," I said, gathering my wits.

"Yes, I've contacted the Mary Therese Fredericks Endowment for the Arts. The Endowment Trustees have agreed to fund the exhibition's tour for an additional year. The plan is for the exhibition to tour four more regional museums. The Museum Exhibition Corporation is working with the museums and with the paintings' owners to arrange for the extended loans of the works."

"Really, how wonderful."

"Yes, this will keep the paintings available to the public for another two years," Dirk said.

"Good of you to take such an interest in the exhibition," Mark said.

"Well, I've been fortunate and my passion is early American Art."

"Yes, and there are two Severin Roesen paintings and three Martin Johnson Heade works that have been a particular treat for me to see," I said. "They're two of the premier still life painters in American History. It's incredibly rare to have them available for viewing here," I continued, directing my comments to Mark and Graziella.

"Exactly. People will travel in record numbers to the museums where this exhibit is shown; so it's a win-win situation for everyone," Peter said.

"How is Evan coming along with his painting restoration studies?" Dirk asked Peter. I noticed that Rosa showed a sudden interest in the conversation when she heard Evan's name. Evan was Dirk's 22 year old son. He had just graduated from college, and Dirk had arranged for Evan's apprenticeship with Peter, much to Peter's chagrin.

"He's a bit impatient with the process, but he's learning," Peter replied.

"He was just looking for you, Rosa," Dirk said. Peter and Graziella looked at each other, and Rosa flushed red again.

"I think I will go back downstairs and get some more food," Rosa said.

"I will go with you," Graziella said.

"No, mother. I will be fine," Rosa insisted, with more animation in her voice than I'd heard before. Graziella looked at her husband and raised her eyebrows, but they let the moment pass and Rosa left.

Dirk excused himself, and Peter uncharacteristically snapped at Graziella, "Why did you let her go?"

"I cannot hang onto her all of the time. It will be better for her when she is home again," Graziella replied. Then turning to me, Graziella said, "I am afraid our daughter has had her head turned by Evan and he is not for us."

"He's been pursuing her with flowers, calling at all hours, and it seems he's the only friend she has made here—not good for a young woman," Peter said.

"I suppose with his leasing the miner's cottage on your land it's hard to keep them from seeing each other," I said.

"*Vero*," Graziella said. "Have you ever tried to tell an eighteen year old girl that she cannot see a boy she is, how do you say, *enamorate*? You cannot fight love, but this is not love. When she is home with her old friends, she will forget him."

Graziella and Peter looked at each other, then Peter said, "I talked to Evan myself and asked him to stop pursuing our daughter. He told me he planned to marry her, and I should just leave them alone or he would talk to his father."

"Talk to his father? What did he mean by that?" Mark asked.

Peter raised his eyebrows and nodded. "What indeed. As Karen knows, Dirk carries a great deal of influence with the GAM Board, which renews my yearly contract," Peter said in a lowered voice. "Not to be melodramatic, but it seemed like he was threatening me, or at least my job."

"Did you tell Rosa about this?" I asked, looking at Graziella.

"We think it is best to just remove her from this person. It is time for her to be in school again soon. She will leave in one week's time."

"What does Rosa say about leaving?" I asked.

"We have talked about it, but she does not know the decision has been made. We will tell her in a few days, with just enough time to pack. This will be the best and she will forget it all when she is home again," Graziella said.

There was a moment's awkward silence.

"Well, we'd better circulate a bit," I suggested.

"Yes, you have many guests looking to see you," Graziella said.

The four of us stood and went our separate ways as couples.

"Trouble in River City!" Mark said as we walked to the bow again. I couldn't help smiling at his choice of words.

"Yes, more than I realized. I knew Peter didn't get along with Evan, but I didn't know why until now."

"Maybe the whole thing will blow over when Rosa's gone."

"Maybe," I said.

Twilight tinged the clouds with pinks and oranges, and the water took on a silvery glow. A steady stream of guests stopped by us to say hello, congratulations, and thank you. This didn't give Mark and me much time to talk, but at least Mark was seeing some of the most beautiful scenery in the country, and maybe getting a glimpse of why I loved it out here so much.

As we stood looking at the sunset reflecting in the River, Lois Fretmeyer, the curator of GAM, came, almost running, up to the rail of the boat. Her hurried pace caught my attention and I watched as Evan ran up after her. He put his hand on her shoulder and spun her toward him. Her face was flushed and they had an exchange I couldn't hear, even though I admit I tried. Then Evan left, and Lois stood staring out at the water by herself.

A few minutes later I noticed Dirk standing next to Lois, whispering into her ear. At this point she caught my eye. I thought she was going to say something to me, but instead, she turned and ran down the stairs. I couldn't shake the feeling that she was trying to tell me something, and I almost followed her. When we were working together on the *Flowers in Art Exhibit,* I'd seen Evan and Lois interact, and I gathered that she was quite taken with him. It didn't appear that he returned her sentiment, and I assumed the scenes I had just witnessed related to this unrequited love. That Dirk was involved seemed a bit strange, but Dirk and Evan had a particularly close relationship, and I figured Dirk was just trying to keep things on an even keel for the sake of GAM.

My musings were interrupted by Polly, who joined Mark and me. She had the Conans in tow. Marge and Henry Conan were in their sixties and seemed to look more and more alike as they aged. They both had thin, close cut grey hair—hers just a bit longer than his. They both wore tweed jackets, khaki slacks, and shoes that could best be described as comfortable.

"It's so good to see you!" I said, smiling and giving Marge and Henry each a hug and kiss.

"Wouldn't miss it for the world, Karen! We're so proud of you and all you've done, dear. And your parents would have been proud of you, too!" Henry said.

"I don't think you've met Mark," I said.

"No, I don't think we've had the pleasure," Marge said. "Although, I've heard a lot about you."

I blushed and continued the introductions, "Mark, Marge and Henry Conan. Marge and Henry, this is my friend, Mark Jordan."

Turning to Mark I said, "Marge and Henry were friends and colleagues of my parents at Beloit College. We've known each other for what—30 years now?"

"You were 16 when we came to Beloit," Marge said.

"They're on the Turning Points Board now, and they're both professors emeritus at Beloit."

"Yes, we've watched Karen grow up into this wonderful young lady," Henry said.

"Thank you for the 'young,' Henry," I said, laughing.

"It's all a matter of perspective, dear," Marge said, smiling.

"I think it's time to start our presentation, Karen," Polly said. "Why don't you go below, and I'll shoosh everybody down there. The band is all set up and ready to start as soon as we're done."

"I'm ready. Do you know where Bella is?" I asked.

"She's already down there talking to the guests and, I think, booking a few engagements!"

"Great! So, let's go!" I said, and we proceeded down to the salon, leaving the darkening sky behind.

As I walked into the salon, Lois Fretmeyer approached me. "I need to talk to you," she said, a look of urgency in her eyes. I couldn't imagine what she would need to talk to me about now. But there was an air of panic about her that made me think it was important. "We're just about to start the award ceremony. Tell you what, I'll meet you on the upper deck, at the bow, in 20 minutes, all right?"

"All right," she said and disappeared back into the crowd.

I walked up to the stage. The band's drum set and microphones were at the back of this platform area. I took a microphone from the stand and flipped on the switch. "Testing, testing."

My voice echoed in the enclosed room. The hum of conversation trailed off as people looked around to see what was happening. "Good evening. We're going to begin our presentation ceremony, so everybody, please find a seat."

Mark selected a front row seat. About half the ten rows of chairs were already occupied. Polly walked through the crowd inviting people to sit down. She joined me at the microphone, clinked her glass with her rings, and invited the rest of the guests to join us. In a few minutes all of the seats were filled, and Polly introduced me.

My remarks were much as you'd expect. I thanked Polly and the Board, expressed my congratulations to Bella, and explained the symbolism of the trophy. It was in the shape of a crystal key to represent the key to happiness: pursuing your dreams in work you love. Tears rolled down Bella's checks as she accepted the award. She hugged me with one arm and held the crystal sculpture high with the other.

Just then, Graziella rushed in shouting, "Peter! Peter has fallen! He is in the sea!"

"What! Graziella, what do you mean?"

She was gasping for breath, her eyes opened wide, her arms waving about her. "Stop the boat. You must stop the boat!"

"Graziella, are you saying Peter has fallen off the boat into the River? How could he?" I asked. My mind flashed on the narrow platform at the bow of the boat.

"*Si*! Yes! He is in the water. We are losing him. Stop the boat!" She was crying now.

"Oh my God," I gasped looking around for a crew member.

Mark jumped up from his seat, saying, "Don't worry, we'll stop the boat. We'll find him! I'll go tell the Captain. Stay with Graziella," Mark said, then sprinted for the door. People gasped and looked around, incredulous.

Minutes later the *Mississippi Lady* slowed, made a wide arc, and returned down river. Then we stopped.

The Captain's voice came through the loud speakers, "Ladies and gentlemen, a guest has fallen overboard. Please stay calm and keep your seats. The Coast Guard has been called. They'll be here very soon."

Every passenger had already rushed out into the cold evening air and crowded the railings. A broad light from the top of the boat swept the River. The light glanced off the water and across the shoreline as everyone on the boat strained to find someone in the water. I looked around for Lois but it was impossible to find her in the press of the crowd. With Peter's falling overboard, I wasn't in a frame of mind to discuss GAM politics anyway, and I assumed that's what she wanted to corner me about.

Graziella and Rosa were standing at the railing. Rosa was crying hysterically, and Graziella, standing behind Rosa, had her arms around the girl's shoulders.

After what seemed like an eternity, but was probably 15 minutes, the Coast Guard vessel pulled alongside. The two captains must have been talking by radio, because the Coast Guard immediately set to work, shining broad search beams across the water and onto the shoreline.

Suddenly, a woman screamed. Then the scream spread through the crowd. People were pointing at the shore.

The Coast Guard must have seen it too. A small motorboat was dispatched from the Coast Guard ship. I could make out two men in the boat. They stopped parallel to the shore, tossed a large net, and pulled something into their boat.

The motorboat returned to the Coast Guard vessel and was winched up. I decided not to wait for an invitation. As the hostess, I felt I had the right and probably the obligation to find out what had happened. "I'm going to talk to the Captain," I said. Graziella looked at Mark. He nodded and took Rosa's hand. I raced up to the pilot house, Graziella right behind me. I rapped on the door, then pulled it open.

Captain Bellows nodded to us, and continued talking into the radio. "10-4 Coast Guard," he said, and hung up the hand mike. "Ladies, please sit down." Graziella squeezed my hand. We sat on a small wooden bench, and I put my arm around her shoulder.

In a sober voice the Captain said, "The Coast Guard has found a body." Graziella and I were both frozen in horror. In a split second he continued, "No, no, it's not your husband." We both looked up, stunned and confused. "This was a young woman, in her early twenties."

"What!" I gasped.

Graziella fainted in my arms.

Chapter Two

The Search

Mark came into the pilot house just as Graziella was reviving in my arms. He looked at me, stunned, and I explained what the Captain had just told us.

"We'll need someone to see if they can identify the body," Captain Bellows said.

"I'll go." The words were out of my mouth before I'd had a chance to think about the logistics of that.

"Fine," the Captain said. I'll radio the Coast Guard that you'll be coming over with some of my crew.

Mark and I said a hurried goodbye. He promised to stay with Graziella and said Marge and Henry were taking care of Rosa. Captain Bellows radioed a crew member to the pilot house, and I followed him back to the main deck. The Coast Guard vessel was just pulling alongside the *Mississippi Lady*. I saw a crowd of passengers and crew members gathered around a lifeboat that had been lowered onto the deck. Two crew members were already sitting in the 20 foot long boat, one in the bow and one in the stern. Strong arms steadied me as I climbed in and took a seat in the middle. The crew members moved everyone back and a crane like arm lifted us, boat and all, above the deck and swung us over the side. I hung on as tightly as I could as we ratcheted down.

There was no moon. Outside the beam of the search lights the night was pitch black. There was no horizon line in the darkness. I couldn't differentiate the water from the air and panic welled in me. I managed to squelch the panic but an eerie foreboding feeling remained. I hoped Peter had made it to the shore somewhere.

We hit the water with a thud. The engine started and vibrated our boat which seemed to have shrunk in the River. I looked up between the two larger vessels. A ladder was hanging from the side of the Coast Guard boat. I saw the backlit outlines of the crew members looking down at us over the railing. The fellow in the stern maneuvered our lifeboat over to the Coast Guard vessel. The bowman grabbed a dangling rope and cleated it to the front of our lifeboat. Then, he pulled us over to the side of the ladder and pointed to me. I stared at him, then the ladder, then back at him. My stomach lurched. This lifeboat didn't feel very safe but the prospect of leaving it felt even scarier. He pointed at the ladder again and shouted something that was drowned by the sounds of the three boats reverberating off the water. I braced myself. I couldn't just sit there. I felt a million eyes on me.

I grabbed the sides of the wooden ladder with a steel grip and eased myself to a standing position. The boat rocked and I prayed I wasn't going to be the third person in the River tonight. I put my right foot on the first rung. This was the hardest part—at least I hoped it was. I swung my weight onto the ladder and moved my left foot next to my right. Although the boats were stopped, we were rolling in the current.

I forced myself to raise my right foot and slid my right hand up the railing as well. Then the left foot and left hand. I was now definitely away from the lifeboat but not really on the Coast Guard boat. I moved up the remaining ten steps as quickly as I could. Strong hands grabbed my upper arms on each side as I reached the level of the railing. They seemed to lift me in the air as I swung my leg over the side and, thankfully, planted my feet on the deck. I steadied myself and looked back down at the water as the lifeboat disengaged and headed back to the *Mississippi Lady*.

"Captain asked us to bring you up to the bridge, ma'am," one of the crew said.

"Fine. I'm ready," I said. We walked in step to the front of the boat. As we moved along, a large, I mean really large, dog ambled up to us.

"This is Baxter," the man said, reaching down and patting the dog's massive head.

"The Captain's dog," he explained. As we moved on I looked back over my shoulder to see Baxter staring after us. He must have been three feet high standing on all fours. Certainly his head was larger than mine. I stumbled but caught myself and refocused on where I was going.

The Captain's bridge turned out to be in an enclosed area near the bow of the boat. We went in and the crewman introduced me to Captain Ken Kruse.

"Ms. Prince, thank you for coming on board. I know this isn't going to be pleasant," he said. I found myself looking into startlingly clear blue eyes. Why was I noticing his eyes? Must be the shock of things, I thought. Everything seemed to be moving in slow motion, every detail emblazoning itself on my brain.

"It's more of a shock than you can imagine," I said, forcing myself to stop looking at him. "I assume Captain Bellows told you that my friend, Peter Pierpoint, fell off our boat. Have you seen any sign of him?" I asked, turning back to him.

"No, I'm afraid not yet. But we've just begun the search," he said.

"Well, I want to stay with you—while you're searching for Peter. I feel responsible—as the organizer of the trip," I said, my voice trailing off.

"I understand. That's fine with me. Crewman Roberts here will take you to see the body. Then he'll bring you back here. That is, if you feel up to that right now."

26

"I'd like to get it over with. I don't know if I'll be able to identify the person for you, but I'll look." I was hoping against hope that it would be someone I'd never seen before.

The crewman led me below and I began to understand the meaning of the term, "the bowels of the ship". We snaked through narrow corridors and finally ended up in a storage area, every inch of wall space lined with cabinets. There on a long bench draped with black plastic was a form draped in more black plastic. We stood alongside the bench. Two more crew members came into the room, right behind us, and the four of us stood around the black draped form. The three crewmen looked at me.

"Are you ready?" Roberts asked.

"Ready as I'm going to be," I replied.

With that, he lifted the tarp and folded it back to reveal straggled blonde hair and the now ashen face that had only recently been in animated argument on the deck of the *Mississippi Lady*. It was Lois Fretmeyer.

I stared for a moment, gasped, then turned to walk out of the room.

"Sorry, ma'am. But could you identify the body for us?"

"I stopped, realizing that they probably had the crew members there to act as witnesses to the identification. "Yes, sorry, of course. It's Lois Fretmeyer. She was on the *Mississippi Lady* with us tonight."

"Thank you, ma'am. I'm sorry."

"Is that all? Can I leave here?" I asked.

"Yes, ma'am. I'll take you back to the Captain now, ma'am."

I turned away again and walked out the door. Once in the passageway, I grabbed the wall and steadied myself. Roberts grabbed my arm and I struggled to regain my composure. "I'm fine Roberts, thank you," I said, straightening my backbone and walking purposefully back up the stairs to the main deck.

"She was from our party. Her name is Lois Fretmeyer," I told Captain Kruse back at his bridge. "What we need to do now is to find Peter. How do you do that?" I asked.

"I'll radio the *Mississippi Lady* and let them know about Ms. Fretmeyer. I'll send them back to shore, and we'll continue our search out here, Ms. Prince."

"I'm staying," I said.

"Yes, ma'am. You said that, and I'll let Captain Bellows know that as well."

"Thank you. Oh, Captain, do cell phones work out here?" I asked, suddenly thinking of Mark and Graziella.

"Yes, ma'am. They do. You'll get good reception out here. There're towers on both sides of the River. It's quietest in here. The sounds of the wind and waves are blocked somewhat and you're farther from the engines. So feel free to call from in here," Captain Kruse offered.

I felt somehow odd about calling Mark. I didn't know why, but I did. The Captain must have noticed my hesitation because he said, "If you'd prefer more privacy, you can step outside."

"Thanks," I said, stepping away and pulling my cell phone from the bag strapped round my waist. Designers had finally come up with a practical idea for woman's accessories—a purse that left you with free hands. Anyway, I was thankful I had my phone and hoped Mark had his cell on. I moved just outside the Captain's bridge onto the small upper deck surrounding it. I dialed Mark's cell phone number. Three rings. I was just thinking that he must not have it on when he picked up on the fourth ring.

"Mark, it's me. Can you hear me all right?" I asked and found tears welling in my eyes. "It was Lois Fretmeyer. The body they found. It was—she was—the young woman from GAM."

"My God! Karen, how awful. Could you tell how it happened? Any signs of a fight? And did they say anything about Peter?" He rapid fired questions at me.

"She was pretty badly bashed on the back of her head. But I couldn't tell anything about how she ended up in the water. A coroner or someone will have to do that. And no sign of Peter—yet. We're just going to keep looking. I'm going to stay with them out here. I have to. You understand, don't you?"

"Of course. Of course. I wouldn't expect you to do anything else. I'll let Graziella know. The Conans are with us—with Graziella and Rosa and me."

"The Coast Guard is going to send the *Mississippi Lady* back to shore. So, call me when you get back, all right?"

"I will. Karen, I have to be back in the office tomorrow but if you want me to stay here tonight, I will," he said. That was a touching gesture. But I didn't see the point of Mark missing his meetings, especially since I'd be out here.

"No, go ahead. I don't know how long I'll be out here anyway. We can keep in touch by phone. Just be sure someone is with Graziella will you?"

"I will. The Conans have already said they would stay with her. So don't worry about that."

"Good. I'll leave my cell on."

"Me too."

I clicked "end" and stared out at the lights sweeping the water for a few minutes before going back to the Captain's bridge. I figured I could watch better from there, and I'd be able to hear any reports that came in to the Captain.

I took a seat on the elevated chair next to Captain Kruse and resumed following the beam of the search lights. We watched in silence as the *Mississippi Lady* pulled away from us and became only red and green lights moving through the blackness.

"How did he go overboard?" Captain Kruse asked, breaking the silence that had enveloped us.

"Good question," I replied. "We were all in the lower cabin having the award ceremony. At least most of us were."

"Was he drunk?"

"Peter never has more than a glass or two of wine. We'd had a drink, yes, but drunk? No."

"So how did he fall over the railing?"

"As far as we know, no one was with him. Maybe he was leaning over for some reason and the boat lurched, or he somehow lost his balance," I proffered.

"Maybe. Could happen I suppose," Captain Kruse said. "But pretty unlikely. Can't say I've ever heard of someone just falling off a cruise boat like that. And what about the young woman?"

"I don't know. The funny thing was she'd wanted to talk to me downstairs. I said I'd meet her on the upper deck in 20 minutes. I figured no one would be there because it was a bit cold, and really everyone was inside watching the entertainment."

"Did you go up there to meet her?"

"No. I never got the chance. She left and I do think she went outside. I stayed and made the award presentation. Then Graziella came running into the room screaming that Peter had fallen overboard. I didn't really think about meeting Lois, not until I saw her again—here."

There was a moment's awkward silence. We both stared out ahead at the search beam moving rhythmically across the water. Captain Kruse broke the silence again. "Pretty unusual to have two people falling overboard like that. You think they were fighting or doing something together that they both went overboard?" he asked. The idea jarred me.

Fighting? Lois and Peter? Or doing what? I tried to imagine a scene like that but it didn't make sense. "Very unlikely. I mean, so unlikely it's, well, it's impossible. I don't think there was any tension between them, and I just can't see Peter using violence anyway. That just doesn't make any sense. I think there must have been some kind of accident."

"An accident happened to both of them?" Kruse asked.

I looked at him. "I—I guess so," I said, the implausibility of it hit me even as I said the words. "Or maybe to one of them and the other jumped in to the rescue," I said. That sounded more likely to me, knowing the two people.

"Well, the sheriff's office will be talking to Peter's wife. She knew he fell in, so maybe she saw it happen," Kruse suggested.

"Yes, probably," I said. The mention of the sheriff jolted me. The Jo Daviess County sheriff's department had one detective. That was Detective Cavanaugh. We'd met under less than ideal circumstances last October when my friend Alice's husband had been killed. In fact, we'd gotten off to a rather rough start. But we ended up on the same team and saved each other's lives along the way. That kind of thing tends to form a bond. I hadn't had much contact with him since then, which is probably a good thing. But I expected he'd remember me. In fact, I was sure he would. And I figured it'd be better to talk to him right from the start this time.

"Is there a way to reach the detective handling the investigation?" I asked.

"Sure, phone or radio. Either way will reach them," the Captain said, looking at me questioningly. Then he added, "I'm sure they'll be meeting the boat as it comes in and will take everyone's statement before they leave the ship."

I thought of all of our guests. They'd endured the shock of Lois's death, of Peter being overboard, and of being questioned by a detective. What a turn of events!

"Well, if we can reach the investigator, I'd like to try to do that," I said.

"Sure, I'll call," Captain Kruse said, picking up his cell phone. "I'd like to know if the *Mississippi Lady* is back in port now anyway."

I expected he was making up a reason of his own for the call and that one sounded fine to me.

"Hello. This is Captain Kruse of the Coast Guard Cutter *Grant* calling. I'm trying to reach the detective meeting the *Mississippi Lady* at Frentress Harbor. Would you have a way for me to reach him?" A pause, and then, "Great, got it. In fact, if you can patch me in that would be even better."

It sounded like the dispatcher had some sort of three-way calling feature and was putting the Captain through to Cavanaugh. In a few minutes, he was on the line.

"Detective Cavanaugh, this is Captain Kruse, from the Coast Guard Cutter *Grant*."

"No sir, no sign of him as yet, but I wanted to establish a direct line of communication with you, sir. We do have a direct ID on the woman's body we found. It's a Lois Fretmeyer. Ms. Karen Prince just identified the body, sir. Yes, I did say that was Karen Prince. Yes, sir, she's right here with me now. Yes, certainly, Detective. Just a minute," Kruse said and handed me his cell phone.

"Detective Cavanaugh, this is Karen Prince."

"So, we meet again, Karen. How are you?"

"I'm fine, Detective. And you?"

"Fine, Karen, except for being called out here to find one person dead and one missing. What was happening on that boat?" he asked, sounding none too patient.

"We were having a dinner cruise with friends and members of the Museum—a celebration party. I'd rented the boat. I don't know how they went overboard, but I did identify the body. It's Lois

Fretmeyer, curator from the GAM. No question about that. And Peter Pierpoint is still missing. I'm staying out here with the Coast Guard until we find him." I noticed Kruse frowning at me as I said that. Well, I had every hope that we'd be finding Peter yet tonight.

"When do you think my guests on the *Mississippi Lady* will be able to go home?" I asked Cavanaugh.

"I'll be taking a statement from each person on the boat. Their name, number, and where they were, what they saw. How many people did you have on board?

"I expected a hundred, but didn't keep a count of who was there. My recollection is that most everybody that RSVP'd showed up," I said.

"Well, it'll take a few hours then before I get to everyone. I'll release them as soon as they've given their statement," he said.

"Could you do me a favor, Detective Cavanaugh, and talk to Graziella and Rosa first and then the people who still have to travel tonight? I know Polly Andrews and Mark Jordan both have to drive to Chicago. There may be others from out of town," I said.

"I'll do my best to get the people who need to be on the road on their way," he said. "Call me if you find any sign of Peter, would you?"

"Yes, of course," I said.

"And Karen, let's keep in touch. No Sherlock Holmes stuff this time," he said, pointedly.

"No, of course not," I said. "We'll definitely stay in touch." I thanked him and closed the cell phone.

Kruse was looking at me questioningly.

"We were sort of involved in a case together last fall," I said not wanting to go into the details.

"I see," Kruse said, looking at me sideways.

Chapter Three

Late Night on the Water

I excused myself, took my cell phone outside and called Mark again. This time he picked up on the second ring.

"Mark, it's me again. Just wanted to let you know that I talked to Detective Cavanaugh and, although he has to talk to everyone on the boat before they leave, he's going to talk to Graziella, Rosa, you and Polly first."

"Thanks, Karen. Any news from there?" he asked.

"No, unfortunately there's been no sign of Peter yet. What about Graziella? Is she there with you?"

"Yes, she and Rosa are here. Do you want to talk to them?"

"Yes, but first, tell me what she's told you about how Peter fell overboard."

"She doesn't know how it happened."

"What? How'd she know he fell in then?"

"They were in the main salon and wanted to go to the upper deck for a minute to talk. Peter went ahead and Graziella stayed behind to find Rosa and tell her they'd be right back. When she went up a few minutes later she didn't see him on deck and then, suddenly, she saw him in the water. She said she screamed, grabbed one of the life jackets and threw it to him. Then she ran back downstairs to find us."

"So she doesn't know how he fell in?" I repeated.

"No. No idea," Mark said.

"And what about Lois? Did Graziella have any idea how she fell in?"

"No. She didn't see her out there at all."

"Does she think Lois and Peter fell overboard together somehow?"

"She didn't think so," Mark said.

"Very strange," I said. "Very strange."

"It is," Mark said. "Anyway, Bella's offered to take Graziella and Rosa home as soon as we can leave here," he added.

"Oh, Bella! I forgot to mention her name to Detective Cavanaugh. When you talk to him, if you could explain about Bella and the Conans taking care of Graziella, I'm sure he'll talk to them right away as well," I said.

"That should work out. I expect Bella and the Conans will be with Graziella and Rosa when Cavanaugh talks to them, so he'll figure it out. But I'll mention it, just in case."

"Thanks."

"I'm heading back with Polly. She came out here with the Sellers and I promised I'd give her a ride back to Chicago tonight," Mark said.

"That's a long drive. And it's already later than I thought you'd be able to get on the road. I hope they'll be letting you out of there soon," I said.

"I don't think it'll be too long now. Don't worry about us. It's Peter we need to worry about. And I just want them to find out what happened to Lois," Mark said.

"Me too," I said as my thoughts drifted back to Peter. "The River's pretty calm but it's cold. Our best hope is that Peter made it to shore quickly so hypothermia didn't set in," I said.

"Yes—and that you can find him quickly. He might be disoriented from the cold even if he did make it to shore," Mark said.

I didn't like his use of the words "even if." "Hopefully he did and we'll find him soon. Keep your cell on and I'll call you with any news. Can I talk to Graziella for a minute? Oh, and Mark, drive carefully. Let me know you get home, OK?"

"OK. Here, let me give the phone to Graziella."

"Oh, Graziella! How are you and Rosa doing?"

"Terrible. I am so worried about Peter—and—that poor girl. It is truly so awful!" Graziella sobbed into the phone.

I wished I was there to give her a hug and searched for comforting words. "We'll find Peter. Don't worry." But even as I said the words I knew she couldn't help but worry. How could she not? I was worried. That's why I'd stayed with the search party. "Do you have any idea how this happened, Graziella? I mean—how Peter fell overboard?"

"*Non lo so. Non lo so,*" Graziella lapsed into Italian. "Sorry. I forget sometimes to talk in English." She sobbed again. "I don't know. I just don't know."

"Do you think he could have been talking to Lois when this happened? Maybe he saw her fall overboard and jumped in to rescue her."

There was a pause. "Yes. Yes, I suppose that is possible. I have been thinking the same thing. That would be like Peter," Graziella said.

"Was Peter a good swimmer?" I asked.

"*Certamente*! Yes, he was."

"Well, see, that's good. That could have been why he felt he could jump in and save poor Lois." But I thought of the many times I'd heard that strong swimmers drown more often than weak swimmers because their confidence gets them in more dangerous situations. I banished the thought and numbly repeated myself. "We'll find him. We'll find him. Mark tells me that Bella will drive you and Rosa home, and the Conans will stay with you. If you need anything just call me or Bella."

"I just need Peter to be safe," she said and sobbed again.

"I know," I said. "He will be." And I sincerely hoped he would.

With that, we said our goodbyes and I went back into the Captain's bridge. I had Bella's cell number and I planned to call her later when they were off the boat.

It was a long night, alternately staring into the dark waters and the glare of the search lights. The searchers took turns in two hour shifts with the binoculars. I'd been on deck for the past four hours, but had come back in to warm up. I sat on a raised wooden chair next to Captain Kruse and looked out. Now, as the relative warmth of the cabin enveloped me, I drifted off. The stress, the darkness, the rocking—I soon found it impossible to keep my eyes open.

"Why don't you lie down for a few hours?" I heard the Captain say as I jerked myself awake.

"Hmm…No, I couldn't. I couldn't sleep."

"You just were," he said, not taking his eyes off the water.

"No, just nodded off a bit. I'll be all right."

"There's a guest bunk just below. I'll have one of the crew take you there," he said.

"What about you?" I asked. I couldn't imagine how he was staying awake.

"We're all used to this. We take six hour shifts. I'll be spelled here shortly."

"No, I'm fine now. I think the warmth just made me drowsy for a bit there."

"Suit yourself."

We sat in silence for a few minutes.

"Do you think we'll find him?" I finally asked.

"I'd say the odds are good, as long as he didn't run into any barge traffic out here. That's the main danger to a swimmer in this river."

"Those barges are huge," I said. "Do you think they could see a man in the water?" I asked.

"Problem is, even if they could see him, they couldn't stop their forward motion in time to avoid him. They're only moving about five miles an hour but, you know, with a full load it can take a mile for them to stop."

"You're kidding!"

"No. No brakes, you see. They've got a lot of forward momentum going. The tow pushing them would have to go into reverse, and it would literally take them a mile to stop."

"So how do they go through the locks and things like that?" I asked.

"Carefully, with a lot of planning," he said.

I thought about that for a while, then asked, "What do they have in those barges?"

"Oh, just about anything that isn't really time sensitive: coal, grain, quarry rock, anything you'd ship by truck or train," he said.

"Why do they ship by barge instead of trucks or trains then?" I asked.

"It's a lot cheaper," he said. "One barge carries the equivalent of 60 semi-truck loads. And a towboat here on the Mississippi can be pushing 15 barges at once. Think of that. That's the equivalent of 900 trucks being moved by one tow."

"Really, that's amazing!" I said.

"Yup, that tow is moving the same amount as two and a half 100-car trains."

"Do they move through here at night?"

"They move 24 hours a day, as long as the weather's good," Captain Kruse said.

"I don't remember if I saw a barge after Peter went overboard," I said.

"Believe me, you'd remember. Being on the River when one of those big boys is passing you is not something you'd forget. You'd have gotten way out of the way. The barges have to stay in the channel, but smaller boats, like the excursion boat you were on, have a shallower draft and you'd have made way for the tow."

"I don't remember seeing anything like that."

"So there probably wasn't one that we have to worry about. So, if I had to make a guess, I'd say your friend probably made it to shore."

"How cold is the water right now?"

"Well, the ice went out about two months ago, in March. We're warming at about ten degrees a month, so I'd say it's about 50 degrees right now."

"That's pretty cold." I was worried about cramping and hypothermia.

"The River's nearly a mile wide here. You were roughly in the middle, so he had about 850 yards to swim to get to shore. But it would have gotten shallow enough to stand up well before that."

"So you think he could have made it to shore all right?" I knew he'd already answered this, but I just wanted to hear his affirmative answer again.

"He could have. He certainly could have."

The unstated negative possibility hung in the air, and I didn't want to think about that. But it kept coming back to me—he could not have made it as well.

We continued the search into the early hours of Monday morning without a sign of Peter. Then, about six a.m., one of the crew radioed into the pilot house, "I think I have something, Captain. There's something orange dead ahead on the rise on the west shore."

Captain Kruse slowed the engines and kicked them into reverse for a moment to stop us.

"Do you see anyone out there?"

"No, sir. Just, something orange. Might be a life jacket, sir. Looks like it."

"Might just be washed overboard from some fishing boat, or water skier," the Captain said. "But you'd better check it out. Take an RHI and two men and report back, Crewman Taylor."

"Aye-aye, Captain."

When they finished talking on the radio, I asked the Captain, "What's an RHI?"

"Rigid Hull Inflatable. They're easy to maneuver in the River and along the shore."

I could see the crew readying the RHI, and lowering it into the water. There was a light fog hanging low on the water now, just skimming the surface. Pinks and oranges spread across the eastern sky, and the clouds glowed with the rising sun. I watched the RHI being lowered into the water, and held along side the cutter with lines from each end. Three crew members, one of whom I assumed was Taylor, climbed down a ladder into the rubber boat and pulled away.

I watched the search team as they made their way to the shore. There were two trees fallen across the bank, victims of a recent storm. Looking through the binoculars, just to the right side of these trees, I could see a bit of orange. The RHI pulled along the shore and one of the men climbed from the boat onto the bank. I could see him grab the orange object and then look around. He disappeared into the trees for what seemed an eternity, but was probably about five minutes, and then climbed back into the rubber motor boat.

Once back onto the cutter, Crewman Taylor reported in person to the Captain. I listened as Taylor answered Captain Kruse's series of questions:

"No, Captain, no sign of anyone, except for the foot prints and this life jacket."

"Well, Captain, it's pretty sloppy out there. Hard to say for sure, but I think there was only the one person's prints. Man's, I'd say, from the size of the print, and barefoot. They led into the woods on the shoreline. I called but no answer. Might get a tracking team and see if they can pick up a trail there."

"If that is our man and he made it to shore, I expect he'd get to the nearest house and call from there," the Captain said.

"It's a 200 foot climb up the bluff. But there's an access road for a boat launch not too far away. He could have stumbled on that and found a house along there," the Crewman said.

"I think we would have heard if he'd called in, but I'll check with his wife," the Captain said. "Any markings on that life vest?" the Captain asked.

"No, it was just standard issue. Could have been from any of the speed boats on the River, or the fishing boats, or the excursion boat, I suppose."

"I'll call the *Mississippi Lady* and have them inventory the vests and see if they have any markings on their jackets," the Captain said. "Thank you, Taylor. You and the men did a good job. Tell the crew to stow the RHI, and we'll be heading back. The Cutter *Lincoln* is coming out here to take our place and carry on the search within the hour. Tell the men to prepare to return to dock."

"Aye-aye, Captain."

With that, Taylor saluted the Captain, turned and left the Captain's bridge.

"Captain Kruse, when I was talking to Graziella she said she'd thrown a life vest to Peter. That could be it."

He looked at me and I realized I should have told him that earlier. But he just said, "Could well be. Or, he could have grabbed a vest from one of the chests along the deck before he jumped in. But a couple things bother me. Why didn't he alert someone else? That would have been the prudent thing to do. And most of these boats stencil the name of the ship on the jacket. This one is standard issue, like you'd buy at any yachting and navigation store."

"So you don't think it was Peter's?"

"It could have been. I'm just saying it's too early to draw any conclusions yet."

"I can call his wife and see if she's heard anything. He would have called home first, I'm sure."

"Good idea. And I'll radio to the Guard office."

So, while I called Graziella, Captain Kruse radioed the Coast Guard headquarters in Dubuque. Neither of them had heard anything from Peter. He was still out there. Or so I hoped. So we all hoped.

Within 30 minutes the Coast Guard Cutter *Lincoln* had pulled up near us, and we were ready to head back to port.

"How will you be getting home, Karen," Captain Kruse asked.

"Well, I— I haven't thought about it. I guess I'll call Bella," I said.

"Where's your car?" he asked.

"I left it in the lot at the *Mississippi Lady's* dock," I said.

"I'll give you a lift there," he volunteered.

"Well, that would be great, if it's not too much trouble," I said.

"No trouble at all." I go right by there. We're just up on the bluff, overlooking Frentress Harbor."

"You and your family?" I asked. I don't know why I said that, it just popped out of my mouth.

"No, well...yes, I guess so. I mean, it's just Baxter and me. Guess Baxter is my family—my wife passed away two years ago."

"I'm so sorry."

"She bought Baxter for me the year before she died. So, he's pretty special to me."

Suddenly, two giant paws, a large black nose and a pair of attentive dark eyes filled the window of the Captain's bridge door. I had to smile. Baxter must have heard Captain Kruse say his name.

"He thinks you're calling him," I said.

"Good boy, Baxter. Good boy." You mind if he comes in here?" Captain Kruse asked.

"No, not at all," I said. Actually, I was somewhat intimidated by the size of this dog but I didn't have the heart to say no and I hate to admit to my own fears anyway. The Captain reached over and opened the bridge door. Baxter pranced in and nuzzled his master's legs, gave him a loving look and then made his way over to my chair. He sniffed my shoes, no doubt to see where I'd been, then my knees, and then laid his giant head in my lap and stared at me.

"He likes you," the Captain said.

I had to smile. Baxter was clearly looking for some attention. I steeled myself and brought my hand to his head. His long ears were larger than my hands. Baxter let me pet his brow. A large pink tongue reached out and licked my hand.

"He won't hurt you," Captain Kruse said. I took minor comfort from this statement and wondered how the Captain could be so sure. I was used to Truffles, my Norwegian Forest cat, whose tongue was a tiny fraction of this size. In fact, she was not much larger overall than Baxter's head!

The brown eyes got to me. "A ride to my car would be wonderful," I said, smiling and rubbing Baxter's head. "Thank you for the offer."

The Cutter *Lincoln* took up our position and continued the search. We made our way back up river and pulled into port next to the Diamond Jo Casino. It was seven a.m. when we disembarked and nearly eight by the time I'd made it home.

Chapter Four

Monday, Monday, Can't Trust that Day

I made it home on pure adrenaline. As soon as I shut the door, exhaustion overwhelmed me. I sank into my overstuffed chair right there in the living room. The stairs to my bedroom seemed too large a hurdle as I leaned back and shut my eyes. I couldn't remember the last night I'd gone without sleep. Well, except for a few nights in Chicago maybe. Anyway, I was beat. Truffs' silky black form appeared at the side of my chair. She jumped into my lap in one smooth motion. She didn't seem to be holding a grudge for having been left alone last night. She trilled, purred, and curled into a ball. As I petted her head, I saw the blinking red light on the answering machine.

I groaned. "Sorry, Truffs," I said, as I lifted her from my lap and carried her the few feet to the answering machine. I pressed playback and sat back down, resettling Truffs in my lap.

Mark's voice filled the room, "Karen, just wanted to see if you were home all right. It's midnight. Give me a call when you get back. Any news about Peter?"

There was a click, a dial tone and the automated voice of my answering machine chanted, "Monday, 12:31 a.m. Next message."

There was another click, and then Bella's recorded voice said, "Karen, it's Bella. I just dropped off Graziella and Rosa. What a night. I'm going to get some rest and go back over there in the morning. Call me."

I put my feet up on the ottoman. Truffs settled down. My head drifted back again and I stared at the ceiling. What a night all right. That was the last thought I remembered until the phone jarred me awake two hours later.

The Caller ID announced "Dara Brown." Through my grogginess I recalled that I had a meeting at the GAM today with Dara and the Galena Gazette. They were doing an article on the upcoming exhibit, and we'd arranged a sneak preview and an interview. Ughhh....

"Dara, good morning," I said trying to sound awake.

"Oh, Karen, you must have one of those gadgets. That, or you're psychic."

"Wish I was, then I'd know what happened to Lois and Peter."

There was a moment's silence as we both thought about that. "So you didn't find Peter last night?" she asked hesitantly. "I haven't heard anything," she said.

"There isn't anything to hear. At least there wasn't when I left at seven this morning. We found a life jacket on shore, but that doesn't necessarily mean anything. It may well not even have been from our boat," I said.

"Do you think the Museum ought to contact Lois's family?" Dara asked.

"I imagine the sheriff's office has done that already, but yes, as her employer, and especially since this happened on a semi-work related event, I think someone ought to call them," I said.

"With Peter gone," she paused, "I mean, missing, we need an acting CEO," she said.

"It would be up to the Board to appoint one," I said.

"I know. I've talked to Dirk, as Chairman, and he asked me to poll the Board." She paused, and I felt my stomach tighten. "They want you to step in until Peter's back," she said. "Would you, Karen? No one knows the Museum and especially this exhibition like you do. I know it's a lot to undertake but, please, would you?" she asked, in a pleading tone. I knew Dara had worked very hard on this exhibit, and it was a large undertaking for a small regional museum. We expected crowds from throughout the Midwest since some of these works had never been exhibited outside their private collections and weren't likely to be seen in this region again in our lifetimes.

I hesitated and Dara rushed on, "Karen, let me be frank. Dirk wants Evan to step in and take over for Peter. That would be a disaster. He doesn't have the experience or the skill to do the job. I pushed the Board to you."

Great, I thought. Now I'd not only be stepping into this role without preparation or any transitional advice from Peter, but I'd have a political battle with the Chairman, and all this in the midst of the largest exhibition this museum has ever undertaken. This was beyond challenging. This was insane.

"Dara—" she cut me off. I guess she could tell by the tone in my voice I wasn't heading in the direction she wanted.

"Karen, who else is going to be able to handle this? We need you," she said.

Against my better judgment I said, "All right." I rubbed by forehead just above the bridge of my nose. This tingling often presaged some dramatic event. I exhaled and wondered what I had just gotten myself into. "What about our meeting this afternoon with the Gazette?" I asked. "Are we still on?"

"I just confirmed with Jonah and he's meeting us there at one. We'll do the tour and then we can discuss the exhibit over a late lunch. I made reservations at The Cookery. Patricia's a wonderful cook and we'll have plenty of privacy for the interview," she said.

"Great. I'll meet you at the GAM. In fact, I'll get there as soon as I can and see what was on Peter's calendar for the day," I said.

"I knew you'd know what to do," Dara said. "See you there at one then," she said and rang off.

I looked at my watch. Ten-fifteen. I figured I'd make my calls on the drive in. The cell phone reception on Blackjack was much improved now that they'd put in the digital towers. I wanted to touch base with Mark, Graziella, Bella and Detective Cavanaugh. Cavanaugh might still be afraid I was going to be poking around in his case again. I had no intention of doing that. At least I didn't at this point. But I had hosted the party where Lois had fallen overboard and died—or been killed; and where Peter had fallen overboard and seemed to have disappeared. I needed to know what had really happened and what the police were doing to find out.

But, I couldn't do anything like this. I scooped up Truffs off my lap, nestled her down in the warm impression in the chair, and headed upstairs to shower and change for the day.

Twenty minutes later I was in the Boxster, heading for the GAM. I had the convertible top up, a shame on a day like this, but I wanted to be sure I could hear on the cell phone. I dialed the Sheriff's Department first and asked for Detective Cavanaugh. He wasn't in, so I left a message on his voice mail and asked him to call me on my cell. I called Mark's office and left the same message on his voice mail.

Next I called Bella but didn't get an answer. I left a message on her machine as well. I expected she was already at Graziella's and I called there.

Finally someone was home. Graziella answered. The strain was evident in the hollow sound of her, "Hello."

"Graziella, it's Karen. I'm so sorry, dear. Have you had any news about Peter?"

"The Coast Guard has just called me. They have not found him yet. And I have not heard from him—." Graziella was trying not to cry but her voice was breaking. "And that poor girl, what happened to her?"

"We don't know yet, Graziella." I told her about the life jacket we found. "You said yourself that Peter is a strong swimmer, right?"

"Yes, he swam in the Adriatic all of August. In Italy, the whole country is on holiday for the month of August every year. We spent that month at the beach, swimming in the ocean and having picnics on the beach," she said.

"He probably made it to shore and we'll hear from him soon," I said, trying to impart a sense of optimism with my voice.

"Yes, let us hope so," she said.

"Please let me know if you hear anything from the Detective or the Coast Guard again, Graziella, all right?" I gave her my cell number. "Graziella, is Bella there yet?" I asked.

"Yes, she is here. You would like to talk to her?"

"Yes, please," I said, and waited as Graziella handed the receiver to Bella.

"Karen, it's Bella. Any news about Peter?"

I repeated the brief story about finding the life jacket. Then I added, "Bella, I've been thinking about something. When I saw Lois last night, on the Coast Guard Cutter I mean, she had a huge gash on the back of her head. I don't know if that happened when she fell in the water or if that was why she fell in. You know what I mean?"

"You think someone hit her on the head and pushed her overboard?" Bella asked, shock registering in her voice.

"It's possible. It would explain how she got into the water. I just keep thinking those rails were really high. It wouldn't be easy to just fall overboard," I said.

"I suppose," she said. "And if that's the case, then Peter could have tried to stop whoever hit her and ended up in the water as well,"

Bella posited. This sounded like a pretty good working hypothesis to me.

"Yes, definitely possible," I said, but something was bothering me.

Bella must have heard it in my voice because she asked, "What? What are you thinking?"

"It's just that Peter didn't tell anyone else he was jumping overboard. No yells, no dogs barking in the night."

"Well, maybe he didn't want to waste time running to find someone. Remember, everyone was downstairs with the music going on. So it's unlikely anyone would have heard him if he screamed. Maybe he just grabbed a life jacket and jumped in," Bella said.

"Maybe, but how did he think he'd get back on the boat?" I asked.

"Maybe he didn't think that far ahead. Maybe he just saw Lois going down for the count and jumped in," she said. "Maybe he figured he could swim to shore. It's not that far for a good swimmer," Bella said.

"Guess that could be the way it happened," I said.

"It seems more probable that they went in the water together than that they fell in separately," Bella said.

"Well, we probably won't really know what happened until we find Peter. I figured he swam to shore, but now it's been 14 hours, and I have to say, I'm surprised we haven't heard from him," I said.

"I know. It's really making me worry," she said.

"Well, thanks for staying with Graziella. I'm on my way to the Museum. I just agreed to keep things together there until Peter's back," I said. "If you hear anything, call me there, or on my cell, OK?"

"Will do, and the same with you. Call me if you hear anything," Bella said.

"We'll keep each other posted," I said. "Bye for now."

"Bye."

As I clicked my cell phone shut, I turned left off of Blackjack onto Highway 20, and crossed the bridge leading into Galena. Galena was built along the Fever River, or as we now call it, the Galena River. GAM is on the north end of downtown, just after you cross the bridge. The GAM parking lot is shared with the Galena Gazette, which is located in the old Kentucky Fried Chicken building. The Fever River Outfitters' tall rack of kayaks and canoes stands between the parking lot and the edge of the river. The city just built a new boat landing ramp across the Galena River from the GAM. Kayakers meander up and down this treelined little river, with equipment rented from our local marathoner and all around athlete, Molly Bode, the owner of the Fever River Outfitters.

The GAM is orange brick, designed to replicate the historic structures of downtown Galena. Most of those buildings were built in the 1830's and 1840's during Galena's lead mining boom. When other downtowns modernized their way into oblivion in the 1970's, Galena was still in a hundred-year sleep. As a result, its buildings remained untouched until the preservation boom of the 1980's. Galena jumped on that bandwagon in a big way. Now Galena has the highest percentage of buildings on the Historic Register of any city in the United States, and is the second largest tourist destination in the state of Illinois. That's second only after Chicago. Pretty good for a town with a population of 3,001.

I pulled into the parking lot and found the Museum open for business for the day. Jimmy, the security guard/custodian, stood inside near the door.

"Morning, Ms. Prince," he said.

"Morning, Jimmy. Is anyone else here yet?" I asked.

"Diane's in the office. Just the two of us here," he answered.

Diane is the administrative life blood of the GAM. She's Peter's secretary and assistant.

"Well, I'll be in Peter's office. Let me know when Dara Brown or Jonah from the Gazette arrive would you?'

"Sure. Will do," he said.

We'd hired extra security for the show once it opened on Friday, but at this point, Jimmy was our only security guard. Friday evening would be the Donor's Preview and my presentation. Although I was generally ready for it, I needed to spend some time putting the finishing touches on my speech. I'd spoken about these artists before, of course, and I looked forward to spending some time studying several paintings in particular. But I was getting ahead of myself. Right now, I needed to see what Peter had on his calendar for the day.

I walked through the frosted glass doors marked "Office" and found Diane working at her computer.

"Good morning, Diane."

"Oh, Karen! I'm so glad you're here. I heard what happened on the boat last night. It's so awful! Poor Lois! How did it all happen?"

"I don't know. No one was up there when they went overboard," I said. "At least no one's admitting to having seen them go in. We're hoping that Peter swam to shore, and we'll hear from him soon." But even as I said it, the fact that we hadn't heard anything by now did not bode well. I shook off the negative thoughts and continued, "In the meantime, the Board asked me to keep things moving for the show here and the opening on Friday. I'll need your help."

"Of course. No problem. Just let me know what you need."

"Well, to start, I'll need to look at Peter's calendar. Do you know if he had any meetings scheduled for today?" I asked.

"I think he had the Gazette coming today. I've got it marked on my calendar, Jonah at one. Will you be meeting with him then?"

"I will. And Dara will be here as well. So we have that covered. What else?"

"He was supposed to meet with Zeenie Zacks this afternoon— she's the owner of some of the paintings in the exhibit. Dirk knows her, I think."

"Can you get me her number? I'll give her a call and see what she wanted," I said. "Anything else?"

"Well, he was working on a project with Evan. That's all I know that he had set for today. But his calendar is on his computer. Let's take a look," she said, moving from behind her desk and leading the way to Peter's dark office.

Diane flipped on the light. We both gasped. Peter's office had been trashed! Drawers were pulled out, papers were scattered everywhere.

"I think we'd better call the police," I said, as we both backed out of the room.

Chapter Five

Lucky Charms

This time I had the Sheriff's Department page Detective Cavanaugh. They reached him at home, and he said he'd be here within half an hour.

Diane and I looked at each other in shock. "When was the last time someone was in there?" I asked.

"I don't know for sure. Maybe Friday night or Saturday," Diane said. "The office is closed on weekends, even though the Museum is open to the public. We lock those glass doors," she said, pointing to the ones I'd come through a few minutes ago. "But, I know Peter was working on last minute details for the opening and everything. And I think he worked on Saturday, because he left a note on my desk. I found it when I came in this morning," she said.

"What kind of note?" I asked.

"He just asked me to follow up with the caterers for Friday's reception."

"Did Peter have a key to the Museum?" I asked.

"Sure."

"Anyone else have one?"

"I do. And Evan, I think. And Jimmy, our security guard, of course. Come to think of it, I'd better get you a key since you're filling in for Peter now."

"Yes, I suppose that could be useful, thanks. I assume the Museum was locked this morning when you arrived?"

"Actually, I got here just after Jimmy this morning. He'd already opened up by the time I got here," she said.

Jimmy—I followed the thread through the glass doors and found Jimmy at the security/reception desk. "Jimmy, could you come in here for a minute?" I asked.

"Sure," he said and followed me back into the office area.

"Jimmy, were the doors locked when you got here this morning?" I asked.

"Yes, of course. Why? What's wrong, Ms. Prince? Is something missing?"

"Take a look at Peter's office. Don't touch anything. Just take a look," I said.

Jimmy walked down the hall, peered into Peter's office. "Good heavens! I don't know when this could have happened!" he said, looking from one of us to the other. "I was here Saturday and Sunday myself," he said. "And I didn't see or hear anything back here."

"Was the office area locked all weekend?" I asked.

"Yes. Well, after Saturday morning, anyway. Now that I think about it, Peter was working in here early Saturday. He left before noon and that was it. No one was in the office the rest of the weekend," he said.

"Thanks, Jimmy. Why don't you go back to the reception desk. There's going to be a Detective Cavanaugh here in a few minutes. Could you send him back here?"

"I'll do that," he said shaking his head as he left us.

I didn't want to disturb the scene until Cavanaugh saw it. But, I also wanted to see what files were opened. And I couldn't see just standing there and waiting. I decided that I wouldn't actually touch anything, just take a peek.

"I'm going to look in Peter's office again," I said.

Diane gave me a shocked look. "I won't touch anything," I said as I headed down the hall. I could feel Diane following me.

I stopped outside the office door and slipped on the gloves I had in my jacket pocket. Diane stayed in the doorway as I went back into the room. Files were strewn across the desk and the floor. Two desk drawers were pulled out, and files stuck out at odd angles. I took a closer look. The papers on the desk related to the show. There was a list of donors and the contract with the Exhibition Corporation that had made the arrangements with the paintings' owners for the loan of their paintings for the exhibit. I had no way of telling what was missing—if anything. As I looked at the papers on the floor, a glint caught my eye. I stooped and saw what looked like an inch long gold icicle. I recognized it as the charm that Peter wore on his gold neck chain. At least it looked like the one I'd seen him wear. I'd asked him about it, and he'd told me Graziella had given it to him on their first anniversary. It was supposed to be an Italian good luck charm. It didn't look like it was bringing him very good luck.

I stared at Peter's computer.

Diane broke the silence, "What are you thinking?"

"I'm dying to get into Peter's computer files but I don't want to touch the keys, in case there are finger prints," I said, sighing.

"No problem. My computer is networked with Peter's," she said. "Follow me."

We went to Diane's desk, and I stood behind her as she clicked on the "My Network Places" icon and then the folder marked "Peter." Suddenly I had access to Peter's computer files.

"Fantastic," I said. "Can I sit there for a minute—and check out his calendar?"

"Sure. Be my guest," Diane said scooting her chair back to stand up. "Oh, while I'm thinking of it, let me give you a key to the Museum." She pulled open the top drawer of her desk and lifted out the pencil tray. Taped to the bottom of the tray was a small red envelope. She opened it and extracted a key. "This will open the front door in case you need to get into the Museum this week," she said, rising and handing me the key. She walked to the calendar next to the office door, lifted it and said, "The security system keypad is right here, embedded in the wall. The sequence is 2005. Just punch those numbers in here if you ever need to use your key to open the Museum," Diane said as she replaced the calendar.

"Thanks," I said. I tucked the key in my pocket and sat down in her chair in front of her computer. "I don't know that I'll need it, but it's good to know I have it in case I do. Now, let's look at Peter's calendar." I scrolled through the list of files on Peter's C Drive and saw several that looked promising. I started with his calendar.

Saturday—it looked like he'd worked with Evan in the morning. At least he had Evan's name marked next to the nine a.m. time slot. The rest of the day was blank. Sunday had "Turning Points" written in at two p.m. Today was the Gazette interview at one p.m. There were half a dozen more appointments for the week, all relating to the *Flowers in Art Exhibit*. I printed out a copy on Diane's desktop printer. Then I looked at the list of files on his C drive again.

I tried opening the file labeled "Evan". The computer whirred away but then told me it couldn't find the file. "That's odd," I said out loud. I tried again with the same result.

"What's odd?" Diane asked. She'd been standing a few feet away but now moved closer and looked over my shoulder.

"Watch this," I said as I clicked on the folder labeled "Evan" again. "I'm trying to open this file and the computer is telling me it can't find it."

"Maybe it's been moved. Want me to try to find it?"

"Yes," I said and traded places with Diane again. A few clicks and she had asked the computer to search its C drive for any files containing the name "Evan". The computer churned away, and then gave us a list of five documents.

Diane clicked on each of them and opened a series of windows. "Here, take a look at these and see if that's what you're looking for," Diane said, giving me the chair again. This time she pulled over another and sat down next to me.

The files were memos from Peter to Evan. They were monthly lists of projects for him. The completed projects were moved to the end of the memo, so the document served as a list of work that Evan had accomplished during his apprenticeship with Peter. I printed these out.

"I still don't see the file just named 'Evan'. Is there a way to see if it's been deleted?" I asked.

"Sure," Diane said. "Right click on the 'Norton Recycle Bin' Icon. Left click on 'Recently Deleted', and left click on 'Restore'."

The computer whirred again and a list of documents popped up. Among those was the "Evan" file. I opened it and found myself looking at a letter to Dirk. Wow! This letter should have been typed in bold red letters, all caps. It practically screamed. Peter accused Evan of refusing to take direction, copying art works he had been told not to copy, failing to do assignments or doing them badly. I hit the print button and looked at Diane.

"Was there by any chance a problem between Peter and Evan?" I asked. She evaded my eyes. "Diane, with this letter it's pretty obvious there was, so give me the scoop—could be important."

She turned and looked at me again. "Yes, there was. Evan was the problem. Peter never said anything to the Board, or anyone else for that matter. But it was painfully clear every day."

"What did Evan do?" I asked. "To be a problem, I mean."

"Evan did whatever Evan wanted. He paid no attention to Peter's directions at all. I think he felt he could get away with it because of his father's contributions and his position with the Museum."

I took the letter from the printer and handed it to Diane. "Take a look at this. Do you think Peter sent this letter to Dirk?" I asked.

She shook her head. "I doubt it. It would have been political suicide. And besides, Peter was extremely tactful in dealing with people. I'd say he was just blowing off steam, typing what he wanted to say to Dirk but would never have let himself."

I read the letter again. In it, Peter told Dirk he wasn't going to keep Evan on as his apprentice. Then the letter rambled on, "I won't be a part of this. And I won't pretend I don't know. And I don't care who you tell. Tell the world if you want to." Tell the world what, I wondered.

I printed another copy of the letter to give to Detective Cavanaugh when he arrived.

I looked at my watch—noon. I had a temporary office set up downstairs, next to the curator's office, and the Museum's painting storage area. I wanted to collect my thoughts for the Gazette interview and to contact the people Peter had appointments with for the week. "I'm going to my office and get organized for the show, Diane. Would you let me know when Detective Cavanaugh or Dara and Jonah get here?"

"Sure."

With that, I gave Diane back her chair and headed down the steps to the lower level. This was the inner sanctum. You could only access the storage area from this one stairwell located in the office area. And at that, you had to have a separate key to open the door at the basement level, and then another to access the storage area itself.

The storage area consisted of aisles and aisles of ten foot high shelves. Paintings and small sculptures were stored in numbered bins. Every item was methodically catalogued: its acquisition number, date of acquisition, date of creation, artist, and provenance were all meticulously recorded. My office was next to Lois's, both of which were just down the hall from the storage area.

"Office" might be a bit too grand a title for my space here. It was more of a small cubicle furnished with a desk, computer and phone. But more importantly, everything seemed to be as I'd left it. I'd developed the habit of using yellow legal pads during my law career and the eight and a half by fourteen inch lined pad sat squarely on a neat stack of manila files, just as I'd left them.

As I picked up the legal pad to make a note to myself about Peter's computer files, a plain white envelope fell out from between the yellow pages. My forehead tingled. Maybe this place wasn't quite as I'd left it after all.

The envelope was sealed, and my name was written on the front in blue ink in a hurried script. No return address or any indication of who'd put it there. This was odd—very odd. Thoughts of the Washington DC ricin stories popped into my head causing me to hesitate. But just for a minute. I picked it up. This hadn't come in the mail. And very few people had keys to this part of the Museum. I held the envelope up to the light. It looked and felt like a letter. I decided I was just being spooked by what had happened on the boat and tore open the envelope. It was a handwritten note—from Lois.

> *Sunday*
> *Ten a.m.*
>
> *Dear Karen,*
> *I was hoping to find you here today. I need to talk to you. I saw something last night on Peter's property, in the old mine behind Evan's cabin. I don't know what to make of it. Not sure who I should tell about this, but I know you'll know what to do. I'll see you later*

today on the boat and we can talk then.
Otherwise, if we don't get a chance to
talk on the boat, please call me as soon
as you can.

Lois

So this was what Lois wanted to talk to me about on the boat—whatever "this" was. Why didn't she just call me at home on Sunday morning? Although, to tell you the truth, since I was painting, I probably wouldn't have taken her call. Well, no point in thinking about what might have been. Better just focus on what I could do now. As soon as I'd finished with the lunch interview I'd head over to Graziella's and take a look in the mine myself.

Now you might be wondering what in the world a mine would be doing on rural property in Galena, Illinois. Well, in the 1840's, Galena was a mining boom town. In fact, back then Galena was larger than Chicago. That's hard to imagine, since Chicago is now a city of over 3,000,000. But in 1840, the lead mining district around Galena had a population of 15,000. Thousands of immigrants came here to make their living in the lead mines. In fact, the word "galena" means the ore from which lead is produced.

Anyway, Peter's property is one of several in our area that still has an abandoned mine shaft. One family has even opened their mine to tourists. And I guess I was about to find out what a mine shaft looked like.

Abandoned mines can be dangerous. I've heard stories about four different mine collapses. One of those was right along Blackjack Road. Truck load after truck load of tailings were dumped in to fill the 100 foot deep gaping hole. Tailings are the crushed limestone rocks left over when the "galena" was extracted. After all these years, nature emphatically demanded its return.

There was also a small miner's cottage on Peter's property, not too far from their house. Peter had thought about turning the cottage into his studio, but Evan had insisted that Peter lease it to him while he was working with Peter at the Museum. Evan had done a minor amount of fixing up on the place, according to what Peter had told me. Evan had set up one of the small rooms as his own painting studio. I wondered if Evan would be there when I stopped by the mine. I hoped not. I didn't want to have to explain to him what I was doing, and there was even the possibility that he'd try to stop me. My course of action now decided, I tended to my museum duties.

I made my calls to the people who had appointments with Peter for the week. It was awkward. I didn't know what to tell them and tried to say as little as I could. Some of the people had heard the news and wanted details. Unfortunately, I didn't have any more to tell them than they already knew—at least not yet. I still hoped we'd hear from Peter soon.

I reached Zeenie Zacks at her hotel. I got the feeling she was just looking for some hand holding. She had three paintings in the exhibit, or at least her trust did. She told me that Dirk Quinn was her attorney and that she is the beneficiary of the Willow Trust. She'd taken a special interest in this exhibit ever since Dirk asked if the Trust would loan their paintings to the show. She planned to be here for the festivities on Friday, and I didn't think she had much to do until then. I thanked her for loaning the paintings and set a time to meet with her on Wednesday. She seemed like someone with too much time on her hands and, right now, I didn't have enough.

Diane buzzed me on the intercom to let me know that Detective Cavanaugh had arrived. I grabbed Lois's letter, made my way back through the locked passage and headed upstairs.

Chapter Six

We Meet Again

I emerged from the stairwell into the Museum's office area. Diane was once again standing in the doorway to Peter's office. She was watching Detective Cavanaugh as he made his way through the papers strewn about the floor.

"Detective Cavanaugh," I said, joining Diane in the doorway. "It seems we're meeting under unfortunate circumstances again."

"In my line of work, that's not unexpected, I suppose," he replied, putting down the papers he'd been examining.

"Have you heard anything from Peter?" I asked, hoping against hope that he had.

"I am afraid not. But, I'd give it a bit more time. It's not impossible that we'll find him all right today. He may have made it to shore and passed out," the Detective said. "Or he may have been carried downstream quite a ways and been stranded on one of the islands."

That actually gave me more hope than I'd had before. In fact, the more I thought about it, that was a perfectly plausible explanation for Peter's continued failure to call home.

The Mississippi has huge sandbar islands just south of here. Some were large enough for people to camp on and they often did in the summer. It was too early in the season for people to be camping out, so if Peter washed up on one of those islands, he could have felt too weak to swim to shore last night. Maybe he'd just collapsed there for the night, and today he'd flag a motor boat and call home. Maybe, I thought.

"That could be exactly what happened," I said. "But I'd really like to know how he got in the water in the first place."

"Well, we have a few working hypotheses," Detective Cavanaugh said. "First, and most likely, he may have seen Lois go overboard and tried to rescue her. Or, they may both have gone overboard together."

"How would that have happened?" I asked.

"Well, they may have been arguing, or there may have been a third person involved."

"Arguing? I can't imagine them arguing," I said. "At least not physically—like that."

"Well, somehow they both went overboard," Cavanaugh said.

"I know." I let out a long sigh. I felt terrible not to have connected with Lois on the boat. "You'd better take a look at this," I said, handing him the letter from Lois.

He took a minute to read the letter, then asked, "What do you think this is about?" Detective Cavanaugh's small dark eyes held mine.

"I have no idea," I said, shaking my head. "I do know she was trying to talk to me on the boat on Sunday. She came up to me just before the award presentation, and I was planning to meet her on the upper deck in a few minutes. Before I got there, Graziella came rushing in telling us about Peter. Of course I forgot about meeting Lois in all the commotion. And then—it was too late," I said, my voice trailing off.

"Yes, and then they found Lois," Detective Cavanaugh said, rubbing his huge moustache. "Did you know what she wanted to talk to you about?"

"Well, at the time I remember thinking it had to be about the show. That was really the only thing we were working on together. But, after reading her letter, I see it must have been about whatever she saw in the mine," I said. "And now I'm thinking about something else I saw earlier, on the boat."

"And what was that?"

"Lois and Evan were talking, or more like arguing. I couldn't hear what they were saying. And, to tell you the truth, I figured it was a boy-girl thing and didn't make too much of it. Then, Dirk came around later and was talking to Lois."

"Was there anything between Evan and Lois?" Detective Cavanaugh asked Diane, who was still standing next to me in the doorway.

"Well, she seemed to be interested in him. I don't think he was too interested in her though. Or maybe Evan was just afraid of her old boyfriend. He was a bit scary, I have to say."

"Who is her old boyfriend?" Detective Cavanaugh asked. Diane had our full attention now.

"He was an art student from—oh, I can't remember where he was from, but it'll come to me. It's a little town outside Madison. Anyway, Lois dated him for a while when they were both in grad school in Madison. She broke up with him a year ago, but he kept showing up at events here. He'd just hang around in the corner and stare at her," Diane said.

"Was this old boyfriend on the boat last night?" Detective Cavanaugh asked, looking at me.

"I certainly didn't invite him," I said, my eyebrows and shoulders shooting up in unison. "But I have no idea what he looks like so I suppose I couldn't say for sure if he was on the boat. There was a guest list but I didn't have anyone taking tickets or anything like that," I said.

Detective Cavanaugh stared at me. "So you don't know for sure who was on the boat?"

"Well, it never occurred to me to take people's names as they came on board. I didn't expect any gate crashers. It's not like it's a crowded place that people would just wander on," I said, somewhat defensively.

"But if they knew about it they could have walked onto the boat?"

"I suppose someone could have. We were at the rail greeting people most of the time, but I couldn't say we were there all of the time. And if we were talking—I suppose someone could have walked on without our knowing it," I said.

"Diane, can you get the name of this old boyfriend for me?" Detective Cavanaugh asked.

"I might be able to find it somewhere—maybe Lois has it in her computer address book," Diane said. "I'll go look."

As she turned to go, Detective Cavanaugh stopped her. "Wait until I've had a chance to look at her office first, would you please?" he said.

"Oh—of course. No problem. I'll look later and let you know. I'll know the name when I see it," Diane said, her voice trailing off.

"That will be fine. Thank you. Now, tell me, was there anything unusual going on in Lois's life recently?" Detective Cavanaugh asked, looking from one of us to the other.

I shrugged my shoulders and shook my head. "Nothing that I knew about, except, oh, she was doing some research into her family, wasn't she?" I said, looking to Diane for confirmation.

Diane nodded her head enthusiastically. "Yes, yes she was. And she'd just found her birth family!" Diane said.

"Her birth family?" Cavanaugh repeated. "What do you mean?"

"Lois was adopted when she was very young, a baby, from what I understand. Last fall she'd gotten the idea to track her birth mother. I think there was a new law or something. Or maybe it was a program that she'd watched. Anyway, something got her thinking she wanted to know her real birth parents. She went to the Sisters and started doing some digging. She found out her parents were living not a hundred miles from here. And they were actually married! Her mother and father I mean. And they had a family. She found out she had three siblings she'd never even met before," Diane said.

"Did she meet them?" Cavanaugh asked.

"Yes, she did," Diane said.

"I hadn't heard any of this!" I interjected, suddenly feeling odd man out in the Museum gossip circle. But thinking about it, I really wouldn't have expected Lois to tell me something like that. Our relationship was limited to the operation of the Museum. And I don't encourage gossip, so that's the sort of thing that would have gone right under my radar.

"Well, Lois and I had lunch together nearly every day," Diane said. "So we knew a lot about each other's lives."

"So how did this family take to having her contact them?" Cavanaugh asked.

"They seemed to be very happy about it. The parents were, anyway. It turns out that her mother and father had been dating in high school. Her mother got pregnant and gave the baby up for adoption—through the Sisters, you see. The parents never knew what had happened to her. They went on to college, got married and raised a family. They told her they'd thought about her many times as the years went by, but it seemed like it would be too—disruptive, I think she said, to try to find her. But when Lois found them, they were thrilled."

"How about the kids, her brothers and sisters? Were they thrilled as well?" Cavanaugh asked.

"Two were, one wasn't, was what Lois told me," Diane answered.

"I'd like the names of the family members. Do you have those?" Cavanaugh asked Diane.

"No, I don't, but I'll bet I can find those in Lois's office too," she said. "Or if not there, then maybe at her house, but I know she has them—or, had them," Diane said.

"I'll be done here in a few minutes and then we'll go to her office. Don't let anyone in there until I've cleared it, all right?" It was a directive, not a question.

"Her office is downstairs and the stairwell is locked," Diane said. "The only other one who has a key now is Jimmy, and I'll go tell him not to let anyone in there," Diane said, leaving us alone in the office area.

"So, will you be in charge of this case?" I asked Detective Cavanaugh. "I mean, with everything happening on the boat—how does that work?"

Cavanaugh glared at me. "The way I look at it, this young lady was a resident of Jo Daviess County. That boat was docked in Jo Daviess County. So it's a Jo Daviess case—my case. I'll work with the Coast Guard, or any other Fed that thinks they should be involved. But if someone in Jo Daviess is killed, I'm involved." He was so adamant that I wondered if there'd already been some territorial claims made.

"Fine with me. I was just wondering if I need to be giving copies of all these documents to the Coast Guard," I said holding up Lois's and Peter's letters. As I did this, it occurred to me that I hadn't yet told Cavanaugh about Peter's letter to Dirk.

"You can ask them that. Just be sure to let me know if anything else comes up," he said, looking me square in the eye.

I got the message. On our last encounter, I'm afraid I'd set some things in motion without telling Detective Cavanaugh first. I'd tried to, but he'd been out. And I couldn't just wait around. Anyway, he ended up arriving in the midst of things and, well, that's a whole other story.

"Well, there is one thing I did find, on Peter's computer," I said. I filled him in on Diane and my search of Peter's files via her computer. Cavanaugh glared at me and accepted the copy of the letter I'd printed out.

"I'll be sure to let you know anything I find out," I offered.

"Why don't you just let me do the finding out this time," Cavanaugh countered.

"Of course, of course," I said, and then thought about the mine. What's a girl to do?

Chapter Seven

The Great Galena Cookery

I continued watching Detective Cavanaugh in silence as he sprinkled white powder on the drawer handles, desk top, and assorted other surfaces in Peter's office. I hadn't been doing that long when Jimmy popped into the office area and announced that Dara and Jonah had arrived. I said goodbye to Detective Cavanaugh and Diane and followed Jimmy back out to the galleries.

Dara and Jonah were standing next to the large round fountain in the center of the lobby. They were backlit by the light pouring through the floor to ceiling windows which formed the front wall of the Museum. I squinted as I looked at them.

"Dara, Jonah, so good to see you both," I said hugging Dara and extending my hand to Jonah.

"Good to see you too," Karen. "How are you doing after last night?" Dara asked.

I exhaled audibly. "Detective Cavanaugh is in there now," I said, glancing at the frosted glass door of the office area.

"It's just too awful. And Peter! Has anyone—has anyone heard from Peter?" she asked.

"No—not that I know of, anyway. But I haven't given up on him yet and you shouldn't either."

"Oh, I won't, dear," she said, and gave me a sad smile.

She knew Peter and I were special friends. Maybe it was my role in bringing him back to his hometown. I don't know, but I felt a special bond with Peter and with Graziella, too.

"Let's just focus on getting this show off to a great start for his sake," I said.

"Here, here," Jonah said. "I can assure you we'll give it great coverage. I've planned a full page spread for the Gazette's Encore Art section. It's coming out this Wednesday, so it'll be perfect timing for the opening. The background articles are all done. I worked with Lois on that." There was an awkward pause. "It doesn't seem real, does it?" Jonah asked rhetorically.

"Things like this just don't happen in Galena," Dara said slowly and deliberately, the inaccuracy of the statement weighing on all of us.

"I know. I know what you mean. I can hardly believe it myself."

I was interrupted by my cell phone ringing in my purse. "Excuse me," I said, swinging the black leather bag from my shoulder and pulling open the drawstring.

I rummaged in the bottom of my bag and came up with my little silver phone. Checking the screen, I saw Mark's number and flipped the phone open to answer his call.

I held up one finger to Jonah and Dara, turned and walked a few feet away from them. "Mark, you made it back all right?"

"Yes, and I just got out of my first meeting this morning or I would have called you earlier. You made it home all right too, I gather."

"Yes, but not until eight this morning! I'm running on fumes. There is still nothing on Peter. Right now I'm at the Museum and just starting a tour of the exhibit with the Gazette. Can I call you later?"

"Sure, sure. I'll be in meetings this afternoon, so just leave a message and I'll get back to you."

I laughed to myself at our usual phone games but at least we'd touched base, so I just said, "Great. Thanks for understanding. I'll call you after lunch then."

When I turned to rejoin Dara and Jonah, I found they'd gone. I looked over at Jimmy behind the desk and he pointed to the main gallery.

Walking into the room, the 22 paintings in the exhibit brought the room to life. I still marveled at the joy and wonder these works imparted. They carried the same impact they had when they were painted, some of them 300 years ago. I joined Dara and Jonah at the first painting. This was a work by my personal favorite, Rachel Ruysch. This piece was on loan from a collector in New York. The work was insured at $8 million and would probably bring more than that if it was ever sold. But it wasn't likely to be. There were four paintings by the Dutch masters and 16 by American floral masters: among them, Martin Johnston Heade's *Magnolias in Bloom* and his *Orchids and Hummingbirds*. Heade's painting career began in the 1840's, the same time that Galena was coming into its heyday. Then there were three works by Severin Roesen. Roesen was a German artist who came to New York in 1848. His works were sought by American collectors then and continue to be highly valued today. Roesen's canvasses are a veritable fount of bounty, featuring large bouquets and tables overflowing with ripe fruits.

As we walked through the gallery I gave Jonah a brief background of the artists and the period their work represented. When we came to the third Heade, something about the painting bothered me. It was one of his studies of cut flowers in a glass vase. I'd studied this work ten years ago, when the National Gallery in Washington DC had a retrospective of Heade's work. This was only the second time this painting had been on exhibit to the public. I'd spent hours at the DC exhibit. Now I couldn't put my finger on it, but something was troubling me about this painting. We continued the tour, looking at two Van Huysum's and a Bossecart. In a small alcove off the main gallery, we had two pastel works by Laura Coombs. Her work was now in great demand. Because of the fragile nature of the pastels and the sensitivity of the paper to light, we had these displayed in a dimly lit alcove off the main gallery. Pastels are basically ground pigment without binder. That's why the colors are so intense. There are no additives to dull them. However, it also makes them more fragile. The first piece featured three stems of deep blue delphiniums contrasted with a spray of pink fairy roses. It was glorious. The second was a bouquet of yellow trumpet daffodils, white jonquils, and purple irises. The work exuded spring's vitality and hope.

"Well, Galenians, tourists, the whole Tri-State area is in for a rare and wonderful show," Jonah said.

"I hope people take advantage of this opportunity," Dara added.

"Oh, I think they will. There've been press releases sent to museums and newspapers in a 200 mile radius. Scholars and collectors will be coming in from all around the country," I said.

"And Friday night is the gala reception, right?" Jonah asked.

"Right," I said. "And now that you've seen the show, how about continuing this conversation over lunch?"

"Yes, I have reservations for us at The Great Galena Cookery. We'll have the place to ourselves and Patricia's promised us something special," Dara said.

We walked the three blocks to the restaurant. It was on Spring Street and the walk there was mostly up hill.

"Well, we'll be ready for a good meal when we get there," Dara said.

"Yes, but it's not as bad as the walk from Main Street to Bluff Street," Jonah replied. "I've often thought we ought to have an escalator going up from Main Street to Bluff Street. You know, there are 192 steps on the stairway in the middle of town. I suppose people used to use them regularly when they were first built."

"I think folks must have been in better shape back then," I said.

The stairs Jonah was talking about connect the main shopping district with the homes and churches on the higher street overlooking town. Jonah seemed to be a born jabberer and he prattled on as we made our way to lunch. I appreciated the distraction.

A few minutes later we were seated at Patricia's table. We spent the next hour talking about the evolution of floral art in America, as well as the events planned for the three months the exhibition would be at the GAM. Patricia had made one of my favorites, her richly spiced lemon chicken picatta served with sautéed spinach and garlic.

As we finished our lunch, our conversation returned to Peter and Lois. It was hard to think about anything else. "You know," Dara whispered, leaning closer to us, "I have a pretty strong idea about what happened on that boat last night." Jonah and I both looked at her. Dara had our full attention.

"What? What do you think happened?" I whispered back.

"I saw that strange fellow who's always pestering Lois. He was there. I saw him in the parking lot by the boat before we went on board. It had to be him!" Dara said.

"Who? When? What are you talking about?" Jonah asked, going quickly through the classic "W' questions of every good reporter.

"You mean Lois's old boyfriend?" I asked.

"Karen, you saw him too?" Dara said.

"No. Actually, Detective Cavanaugh and I just learned about him from Diane this morning."

"No! That's not right! I told Detective Cavanaugh about that young man last night, when we were interviewed before they let us off the boat!" Dara said.

"You did?" I said, my mind flashing back to Diane's comments about Lois's boyfriend. I guess Cavanaugh hadn't outright said this was news to him. I'd just assumed it was. Detective Cavanaugh was certainly playing his cards close to his chest! But, I guess his job is to gather information, not to give it out. My train of thought was halted by Patricia's offer of fresh brewed coffee.

"I'm sure Detective Cavanaugh will follow up on your lead," Jonah reassured Dara. "We can leave it to him."

"Maybe," I thought. "Of course," I said.

Patricia poured the coffee and presented us each with a plate of her spectacular chocolate shortbread torte.

"Thank you, Patricia. Chocolate is my favorite dessert. You know, I'll have to introduce you to my friend, Bella Donna. With what you both do with food, I think you'll have a lot in common," I said.

"I'd love to meet her. She's opened the catering business in The Red House on West Fourth Street, hasn't she?" Patricia asked.

"She has indeed. And she has her recipe book, *Bella's Best*, coming out this summer," I added. It's filled with her ancient and wonderful Italian recipes.

"Really, how exciting! I'll have to get an autographed copy for my cookbook collection," Patricia said.

"Yes, and I'd love to do an interview with her," Jonah offered.

"Great!" I said. "I'll let her know that, Jonah. I'm sure she'd be interested."

After lunch we said our goodbyes and I headed straight to Peter and Graziella's. The mine was still on my mind.

Chapter Eight

The Shaft

Leaving town, I headed out on Blackjack and took a left on Rocky Hill. I drove past the old red brick buildings that housed the county Poor House back in the 1860's. They still stood there, the occasional subject of a redevelopment plan that has yet to take place.

I took another left and was now on Irish Hollow. As its name implies, Irish Hollow was settled by the Irish miners. The road winds through the center of a ten mile long valley or "hollow" as they're called out here. Actually, this is one of the prettiest spots in the county. Just this past year, it was saved from devastation when it was removed from the short list of locations for the upcoming Highway 20 Bypass. Long Hollow won the honor. Good for Irish Hollow, woe to Long Hollow. Such is the price of progress, I suppose. I looked around at the plowed fields and budding trees. I hoped to enjoy this little bit of paradise sans much "progress" for years to come.

This time I was cruising with the top down on the Boxster. The spring sun felt warm even though the air was cool. The long hanging branches of the willow trees lining the streams had gone from their spring yellow to bright green. The apple trees were in blossom, and two bluebirds flew across the road ahead of me. A red tail hawk circled above. Peter and Graziella's property was just two miles ahead.

I drove up the long gravel drive to the two story square farm house Peter and Graziella called home. This style of home was built in the 1860's and was often called a four square. The name referred to the shape of the house: two stories, with four square rooms on each level. The main floor held the entry parlor, living room, kitchen and dining room. A central staircase just inside the front door led up to four bedrooms. Graziella loved the home and always said it reminded her of the farmhouses near her own home in Morrovalle.

I parked in the gravel drive, walked to the front door and rang the bell. Bella answered the door and greeted me with a worried look and a hug.

"Karen, any news?"

"No—nothing that I've heard. I guess that means you haven't heard anything here either?" I said.

"No, and Graziella is getting hysterical. She's getting worse as time goes on and we don't hear from him," Bella said.

"Well, that's only natural, I suppose. I mean, last night, even this morning, she would have been worried but probably still expected that he'd be all right. Not hearing from him—well, it's got to be getting harder," I said.

"Yes, it is. It—well, you want to see her, come in."

I stepped into the parlor.

"She's in the living room," Bella said, *sotto voce*, as she led us into the next room. "And Rosa's in her room, upstairs."

I followed Bella through the small parlor and found Graziella sitting in a rocking chair staring at the phone on the end table beside her. She looked up as we came into the room.

"Oh, Graziella," I said. "I'm so sorry you are going through this. Has the Sheriff or the Coast Guard called with any news today?"

"The Coast Guard called. The life jacket was from the boat we were on last night. They had just bought them for the season you see, and there was one missing, and—" Graziella began crying quietly.

"I know, I know," I said. "But you mustn't give up hope. I was just talking to Detective Cavanaugh, and he said maybe Peter was on one of the islands in the River. I think the Coast Guard is probably searching them right now." I certainly hoped they were. It seemed so obvious once Cavanaugh had suggested it. In fact, I decided I would try to reach Captain Kruse myself and see what he'd heard.

Graziella brightened momentarily. Then seemed to cloud over again, "Yes, maybe, but then what about the life jacket?" she asked.

"Well, he could have let go of that, or lost hold of it somehow, and still be on one of those islands," I said. I didn't like the fact that we'd found the life jacket without Peter either, but it wasn't dispositive of anything, so no point in drawing any conclusions from that.

"How is Rosa doing?" I asked.

"She's upstairs," Graziella said. "She won't eat anything."

"Graziella, can I go out and take a look at the mine?" I asked

"The mine? But what do you want there?"

"I found a note at the Museum—a note from Lois, saying something about the mine was bothering her."

"The thing that was bothering that poor girl was that boy, the one Peter rented the cabin to," she said.

"You mean Evan?" I asked.

"Yes, he was an obsession with her. She was so young, so impressionable," she said.

"Well, if it's all right then, I'll just go and take a look. I'll be right back. I'll take the ATV if that's OK," I said.

"Go, go. It is fine. I will be here," she said, and drifted back to staring at the phone.

I went out the back door and walked the 30 feet to the barn. Peter had two old ATV's (four-wheel all terrain vehicles) that we'd toured his 80 acres with many times. The miner's cabin and the mine were a good half mile from Peter and Graziella's house, and there was a separate driveway to access the cabin. I could have taken the car and driven along the road, but it was quicker to take the trail through the woods to get there.

I pulled on the barn door's worn metal handle. No luck. The door's hinges had rusted and become misaligned over the years. But I lifted up a bit on the handle and managed to swing the large wooden door open. Inside, the barn was dank and dark. A small pattern of light fell on the earth floor just below the sole small west window. The ATV's were parked near the front, and I hopped on the blue Honda. I turned the key, switched on the choke, depressed the brake with my right hand and pressed the red start button with my left thumb. Despite the fact that this machine was at least 15 years old, it started right up. I pressed the inch long gas lever with my right thumb and rode noisily out of the barn.

The trail from the barn to the miner's cottage started as a mowed ten foot swatch in an open field of prairie grasses. By late summer the big bluestem grass would be six feet high and form a tunnel around the trail. Peter kept this trail mowed with a blade attached to the back of the ATV. But this time of year, the grass was not even a foot tall. I bounced along the uneven ground bracing my legs to absorb the shocks. In about a half mile I ran out of field, and the trail went into the woods. This was a mature oak hickory forest. The new green leaves of these broad leaf sentinels formed a canopy over the trail. In another quarter mile I came to a rock outcropping. Giant limestone walls formed a cavern of sorts. I slowed the ATV as I rode through this darkened space. Once through the cavern, the trail swung down to a stream. The log miner's cabin had been built near the stream, next to the old mine shaft.

I stopped the ATV and parked it on the cabin's gravel driveway. I didn't see any sign of Evan. His jeep wasn't there but I knocked on the cabin door anyway. No answer. I knocked again, this time calling out and rapping on the window as well. No answer. Hmmm. I tried the door knob. It turned. I poked my head in and called out again. As long as the door was open, I stepped in to take a peek.

The cabin was small and dark. Evan didn't seem to be up for any housekeeping awards. Papers were strewn across most of the flat surfaces. I called out again as I made my way through the living room and into the kitchen. It had been fitted with semi-modern appliances. A stove, refrigerator, sink and table took up most of the space. There was a small bath off the kitchen. This had obviously been added long after the original construction. The bathroom connected through to the bedroom which connected back to the living room. I was back in the room I'd first entered.

I took a quick look at some of the papers scattered around. There were drawings, sketches of some of the paintings in the exhibit. Well, that made sense, I guess. Evan was in a painting apprenticeship with Peter. A colored study caught my eye. This was a pastel study of one of the paintings in the exhibit. It was a copy of the Heade, *Flowers in Glass Vase,* that had troubled me at the GAM this morning. Funny that this same painting should grab my attention again. I felt a tingling sensation in the center of my forehead, just between my eyes. I rubbed it away.

Lois had said she'd found something in the mine. I decided to see if I could figure out what it was. I left the cabin, closing the door after me and making sure I left it the way I'd found it—unlocked.

The entry to the mine shaft was surrounded by a wooden structure, sort of like a small shed. The front wall consisted mostly of two doors hinged at the sides that swung open from the center. There was a rusted latch that held the two doors shut. And, unfortunately, there was a padlock on the latch. Darn.

I walked around to check out the sides. The walls were weathered wood. If it had ever been given a coat of paint, that paint had worn off long ago. I found a small window and peeked inside. The only light came from this window and a matching window on the other side. It looked like there was a table and chair, and—it looked like there was an easel! How very odd. I had to get a closer look. I made a quick circuit around the building, looking for the best entry point.

At the back of the building a section of the wood was rotted away at the base. Animals had gnawed on this over the years. Maybe they wanted to take shelter in there. Maybe they were just curious like I was.

I scrunched down and took a look at the hole. This was definitely an animal passageway. They'd worn a smooth path in the dirt. The hole was about a foot wide and a foot and half tall, edged with teeth markings. How much wood could a woodchuck chuck? I wiggled the boards and considered my options.

Lying on the ground, I scooted my head through the hole, trying not to think "hunta virus." My shoulders just fit. I pulled myself along wishing I hadn't eaten that chocolate dessert at lunch today. But things seemed to compress enough to let me through.

I got to my feet and dusted myself off with a few slaps at my jeans and the left side of my jacket. There was an easel in here all right, but no painting on the easel. There were a few wooden planks laid as an impromptu floor. They formed a walkway around an opening in the middle of the floor. There was a wooden railing around the opening. This had to be the actual mine shaft. There were stairs leading down. I grabbed my keys from my pocket and flicked on the small penlight on my keychain. The light was a gift from my friend Wanda, and it was amazing how often it came in handy.

I swung the small circle of light along the worn stone stairs. They went almost straight down, further than the light would shine. I moved the light along the chiseled stone walls. We were at the base of a valley here, and the limestone started just a foot beneath the surface. There was something on the wall to my right that caught my eye as I passed my light over the stone surface. It looked like wax drippings. I shined my light higher along the wall, just at the level of the first few steps. A small board had been wedged into a crevasse in the rock. A candle and matches sat on this tiny ledge.

I started down the stairs, stopping on the second step to light the candle. Once the candle on the wall was lit, I saw a whole stash of candles tucked in the corner where the step met the wall. I picked one of them up, lit it and carried it with me as I descended further down the mine.

About ten feet down, the steps led to a short tunnel which opened into a broader chiseled cavern.   There were two other tunnels leading off of this ten by fifteen foot open area, if you can call a pitch black hole in the ground open. I looked back toward the stairs for a minute, took a deep breath of dank air and peeked in one of the tunnels. The remains of a track ran down this three foot wide by four foot tall pathway. This was probably where they hauled out the lead ore. I walked to the opposite end of my cavern and looked in the second tunnel. This one was the same size. I shined my pen light into the tunnel and saw the edge of something about six feet in partially blocking the tunnel. My heart pounded. I thought maybe it was fallen rock. I banished thoughts of a mine collapse for fear of telepathically generating one. Fear generates some strange thoughts. I took a better look. Whatever it was, it was thin and vertical and looked man made. Not a rock.

I steeled myself with the thought that this mine had been here for 160 years. I fought to suppress thoughts of the mine on Blackjack Road that had collapsed only ten years ago. Well, I was here and I didn't see any falling rock. A few crumbled pieces caught my eye.

"Just do it!" I said out loud. My voice sounded hollow and echoed off the stone. I carefully set down my lit candle and climbed into the tunnel. I made my way hunched over, head tucked, right arm extended, eyes glued to the little beam of my penlight.

Four steps into the passageway the light bounced off a plastic tarp draped over something. I stepped closer and lifted the edge of the tarp. I was looking at the edges of three   painting canvasses!

I moved the first canvas out of the tunnel and set it against the wall just outside the tunnel. I stepped back to get a look at the work—two large magnolias set on brown velvet. I gasped! This was a copy of one of the Heade paintings in the GAM Exhibition! I hurried back and removed the second—a copy of Severin Roesen's Bouquet and Fruit. I looked at the back of the stretcher bars. These didn't look new. In fact, they looked like they might be quite old! Could I be holding the original? I raced back for the third painting, my heart pounding. It was identical to the Heade that had troubled me at the Museum earlier today. I looked at the back of the canvas. This looked like old canvas and stretcher bars as well. It could be that someone was making copies of the paintings using period materials. It had been done before—by art forgers! This had to be what Lois wanted to tell me about.

A noise came from the stairway. I froze. Talk about nowhere to go! My mind raced. I thought of putting the paintings back in the tunnel and tucking myself in the other one. But I didn't see how I could do that without making noise. My heart seemed to echo in my head. I focused on the sounds above me. Scratching sounds—I sighed with relief. An animal—probably that woodchuck. OK. Time to go.

I put the paintings back where I'd found them and made my way out of the mine shaft. I scanned the little wooden structure for signs of my having been there, erased a few tell-tale foot prints, and scooted out through the woodchuck doorway.

I wanted to call Cavanaugh. But what would I tell him? I figured I'd better look at the paintings in the Museum first. Maybe I'd be able to tell if they were the originals. That would certainly make a great deal of difference.

I floored the ATV and held on tight as I bounced my way back to the barn. I had to get to the GAM—fast!

Chapter Nine

Fan Mail from a Flounder

I raced back to the Museum and headed straight to the main gallery. The paintings were museum mounted, which meant they were attached to the wall with locking brackets—one at the top and two at the bottom of each painting. Lois had hung these just days ago. I wondered if she had noticed something about these works that had led to her to the mine—and to her death.

I examined the paintings from the front as they hung on the wall. The works looked good. If they were copies, they were certainly well done. I looked at the Heade that had caught my eye before. It looked perfect. Then it dawned on me. It was perfect. Too perfect. I remember studying this painting at the National Gallery and noticing that the paint was cracked in the thinly painted background. I didn't see that kind of cracking now. It could have been repaired, I suppose. The painting itself was so skillfully done I couldn't have said it wasn't by Heade's hand just looking at the craftsmanship. It might take carbon dating, spectrograph analysis of the paint layers, and expert comparisons of the brush strokes to come up with a conclusive determination. And that would be a huge political mess. The slightest question regarding attribution would cause a ruckus in the art world. It would put the future of the show in jeopardy and probably the reputation of the Museum as well. Who'd want to lend paintings to us in the future if we were going to challenge their authenticity? And there were the other museums to consider. Dirk was working on extending the tour. In fact, he had just said he'd gotten consents from the paintings' owners to continue the tour, hadn't he?

And of course, I would be in the center of this maelstrom. My reputation would be at stake as well. Oh great. How did I get into this mess? Well I couldn't turn my back on it now. Maybe if I looked at the back of the canvass I'd get a clue—one way or the other.

I needed a special tool to unlock the brackets. Lois kept it in her office, locked in a drawer. Maybe Diane would have a key. It was nearly five now, and the Museum would close in a few minutes. I sure hoped Diane was still here.

Charging through the office doors, I caught Diane tidying up her desk.

"Oh! It's you," Diane gasped, a bit startled. "I thought you might be Dirk."

"Are you expecting him?" I asked.

"No, but his secretary called here looking for him. He was supposed to meet with his auditors this afternoon. Apparently he forgot about it. With everything that's happened, she thought he might show up here."

Detective Cavanaugh had just left, Diane said, and she was getting ready to leave herself. I didn't want to start rumors about the other paintings I'd found, so I told Diane I needed to study the paintings in the exhibit for my presentation.

"I need to look at them under Lois's magnifying glass with the light on it. I have to take the paintings off the wall to do that. She kept the tools I need locked in her desk." Diane looked at me questioningly.

"I have a key to Lois's office and her desk. I'll come with you and open them. Then you can lock up when you're done," she said.

We made our way down the stairs to the curator's office. A residue of white powder covered the surface of Lois's doorknob, desk, and computer keyboard.

"Detective Cavanaugh was in here taking fingerprints," Diane said as she inserted the key in the lock of the top center drawer to unlock the desk. "But he said he was through in here."

"Does Lois always keep her office locked?" I asked.

"No, actually she doesn't—didn't," Diane said.   But Cavanaugh asked me to lock it when he left. I don't think he'd mind us getting the security bracket key though," she said.

"No, I don't think he would," I agreed.

Diane took the security bracket key, which looked something like an Allen wrench, from its plastic case in the top right hand drawer. I wanted to look through Lois's files, but I could do that later. On to the paintings now.

"Did you find those names for Detective Cavanaugh?" I asked. "The boyfriend from Madison and Lois's birth parents, I mean?"

"Yes, they're on my desk. Would you like them?" Diane asked.

"Yes, I would. But just leave them there and I'll pick them up on my way out. Thanks, Diane," I said, nodding. I guess my intentions were obvious. Or maybe my reputation from last fall's murder case made Diane think I was going to do some investigating myself. Well, actually, I guess I was. Lois had come to me for help, and I felt I had to do something. And Peter. As the hours ticked by I began to wonder if we would ever find him—alive, I mean.

The possible scenarios were multiplying.   Questions raced through my mind. What if he hadn't jumped in to save Lois? Maybe someone, or ones, hit them both and pushed them off the boat! If it wasn't Evan, maybe it was the ex-boyfriend. Maybe the copies of the paintings in the mine were just that—copies. But why were they stashed away like that? Could it be that Evan was selling copies of the paintings?

I spent the next hour studying the three paintings in the exhibit that matched the ones I'd found in the mine. The stretcher bars were certainly old. The canvasses looked original. The paintings had the signs of aging you would expect, slight yellowing of the varnish, and a few fine cracks in the paint film, but generally in good shape. Except for the Heade. It seemed to be in excellent shape! I searched for signs that it had been recently restored. But a good restoration shouldn't show signs—that was the point of it. I made a mental note to do some research on this piece.

It took me about 15 minutes to replace the paintings on the wall, making sure they were properly secured. I put in a request to my subconscious to work on this whole puzzle. My brain seems to solve problems I can't consciously solve if I just ask it to do it and leave it alone. Then when I'm not even thinking about it, the answer will spring to mind. No telling how long this would take, hours or days, but more often than not, it worked.

Diane and Jimmy had gone home by the time I finished. It was sort of spooky being here all alone. Thank heavens Diane had left the light on in the office. In the center of her desk was a single sheet of white paper with two handwritten names and addresses: Mary Austin Wood and Goth Gorski. Since I was alone in the Museum, I figured this would be a good time to take a look at Lois's office, and maybe Evan's too. I started with Lois's.

There didn't seem to be much paper around. No filing cabinet. Maybe Diane kept all the paperwork. The bottom right desk drawer held a few files. I looked at the labels. Each seemed to be for one of the Museum's exhibitions. I pulled the file for the *Flowers in Art Exhibit* and found copies of the contract with the Museum Exhibition Corporation that had assembled the works for this show. They'd entered the separate loan agreements with the various owners of the paintings and then turned around and loaned the entire exhibit to the Museum. But we did have a list of the owners of each of the works, so that Lois could identify the lenders on the exhibit labels, I suppose. And there was a copy of the gallery sheet for the exhibition. I looked for the owners of the three works I'd just examined. Interesting. All three were on loan from the same owner—The Willow Trust. Wait a minute, wasn't that the name of Zeenie's trust? I made a note to see what more I could find out about the Willow Trust. I always carry a little three inch notebook with me for just this sort of thing.

The limited number of files I found made me think that Lois must have kept most of her records on her computer. I hadn't yet made the jump to the paperless office, myself. But Lois was younger, part of the computer generation. I pushed the power button on her computer and listened to it whirr to life. I anxiously watched the screen as the operating system went through its start up procedures. I couldn't wait to see what I'd find here.

Sure enough, she had a lot more files for the exhibition on her computer. I clicked on the icon labeled "Flowers in Art Exhibition." A dozen folders appeared, including one titled "Lenders." I clicked on that and found a detailed list of the names, addresses and phone numbers for each of the paintings' owners. I scrolled to "Willow Trust" and saw the Founders Bank and Trust out of New York listed as the trustee. John Harris was listed as the trust officer representing the estate. I jotted down his name and contact information in my notebook. A trip to New York might be in order. If I went, I'd be able to visit my friends there as well as my New York gallery.

I double clicked on a few buttons: My Computer, C Drive, and My Documents. I scrolled through the names of the folders of Lois's documents. Two folders jumped out at me: One was labeled "Address Book" and the other "Adoption." I clicked on the "Adoption" folder first, and then clicked on the file labeled, "Mother." All of the entries in this document were dated. Lois had kept a chronological log of her efforts to find her birth mother. I scrolled to the more recent dates. In bold type, I saw the name: Mary Austin Wood. That matched the name Diane had given me, but now I had a phone number to go with the address. The address was in Scales Mound, a small town not far from Galena. I wrote the name, number and address in my little blue notebook after the Willow Trust information.

Reading through the file, I got the story of Lois's year long search for her birth parents. I wondered if anyone had contacted the Woods about Lois. Perhaps Lois's adoptive parents had called them.

Surely the sheriff's office had called her adoptive parents. And from what I'd just read, they had been very supportive of Lois's efforts to find her birth parents.

According to Lois's diary, her birth family ran a very successful business selling, well, selling semen. Animal semen, that is: bull, horse, llama, goat, you name it. I wondered for a minute about how that all got collected. Anyway, their business, Bully for Ewe, was apparently successful enough. But the real money had come with their investments in biotechnology. The family had hedged its footing in the animal reproduction industry by investing in a biotech start-up focused on animal reproduction. That company had gone public during the stock market's meteoric rise in 1997. It had made them a very wealthy family. The two sons ran the original family business. The daughter handled the family investments. From Lois's notes, it seemed that she'd gotten along well with the brothers, but the sister had never accepted her. Lois's impression was that her sister was afraid Lois would get a share of the family business, or worse yet, make a claim against her parents' estate when they died. Lois's birth parents were only in their forties, but Lois's mother had been fighting cancer for several years now and wasn't expected to live a lot longer. Maybe that was why she was so happy to have connected with Lois. Whatever the reason, the two of them had an immediate and strong maternal bond.

I closed that file and clicked on Lois's computer Address Book. I did a search by city and looked at the names in Madison, Wisconsin. There were quite a few entries, which made sense since Lois had done her undergraduate and graduate studies there at the University of Wisconsin. But there was no Gorski. I checked the address Diane had given me for Goth Gorski and saw it was on Main Street in Rainbow. From what I remembered from my law school days, Rainbow was a small town just outside Madison. I mentally penciled in another trip on my calendar. I figured I'd go there tomorrow. Madison was only a two hour drive.

I was relieved I wouldn't have to fly anywhere to track him down. Flying was becoming more and more difficult as airlines cut back on flights and increased security. I understood the reasoning, but it seemed to be a downward spiral for them. To pay for the increased security they had to cut other expenses. The more they did that, the more obnoxious flying became. That led people to fly less, leading to less revenue for the airlines, leading to more cuts in expenses, leaving fewer personnel. You get the picture. Anyway, I was glad I could avoid flying.

I used the Address Book name search feature, typed "Goth Gorski" in the name field and hit enter. Sure enough, his name and address popped up. There was also a company name, "Art Walls," but no number. I added that to the notes in my little blue book. There didn't seem to be anything else about him in the Address Book. I closed the program, and the screen returned to the desktop image of clouds and a half dozen shortcut program icons arranged on the left side.

My forehead tingled, and I caught myself rubbing the area above the bridge of my nose. I took this as a sign I was on to something, I just didn't know what yet. I glanced at the icons and my eye stopped at the Norton Recycle Bin. What a handy little feature. I right clicked on it and a menu dropped down. I read through the options until I came to "Restore Deleted Files". That sounded interesting. I left clicked on that and once again the computer whirred into action.

A window appeared listing two files and asking me if I was sure I wanted to restore them. "By all means," I said out loud, clicked "Yes" and watched the screen anxiously as the progress bar moved from left to right.

"Do you want to open these files?"

"Yes, Yes!" I clicked "Open."

Two windows appeared on the screen in front of me. The first was a letter from Lois to Goth. At first glance, I thought it was a "Dear John" letter. But as I read on, it was more than that. Lois was asking Goth to leave her alone. I looked at the date of the letter—written only two days ago. There was no way of telling if Lois had sent the letter, but it certainly painted a picture. Lois hadn't used the word stalking, but it was clear that that was what was going on. I printed out two copies.

The second restored document was a memo from Lois to Peter. I rubbed my forehead as I read Lois's words. She had serious questions about Evan. She'd come to the GAM late last Tuesday evening to work on the show. The Museum was closed, and she'd been surprised to see the lights on in the gallery. When she walked into the gallery, she'd found Evan and Zeenie Zacks hastily hanging a painting back on the wall. He'd said he was working on a project for Peter. Lois pressed him on the project, and he said he was doing studies of the works as a part of his painting restoration program. He said he examined the works at his desk at night so that he wouldn't interfere with the exhibition. Zeenie was apparently using her position as owner of the paintings to get a behind the scenes look at the GAM and the exhibit. Lois was objecting to having the works handled in this manner without her knowledge. "As curator, I should have been informed and consulted on this use of the works." She must have been very upset to have written this memo. Usually a problem or issue would just be discussed. Maybe she was concerned for her own reputation in the industry and was making a paper trail. Maybe she was just young and inexperienced enough to write to her boss instead of talking to him and working things out. In any event, I wondered if this was what she was arguing with Evan about on the boat. I wondered why she had deleted the document. Was it a draft that hadn't been sent? Or had someone else accessed her computer and deleted it?

I printed two copies of this document as well. Lois's printer was on a small table against the wall next to her desk. As I retrieved the documents I'd just printed, a sheet slipped from my hand. I was getting tired. I bent down to pick it up and saw a manila file folder wedged way back against the wall under the table. Curiosity got the better of me. I pulled it out.

Jackpot! The file was filled with letters from Goth Gorski to Lois. And I do mean filled. No wonder she'd written to him to back off. There were hundreds of letters here—rambling, hand written, expressions of longing. Scary. They dated back over the last year, but most had been written in the past few months. It looked like he was sending more than one a day. I decided to copy some and put the whole file back where I'd found it. Part of me wanted to take them, but that would probably be tampering with evidence. I'd tell Cavanaugh and let him decide what to do.

Chapter Ten

Home Again, Home Again

I carefully locked the Museum door behind me and checked my watch. Seven p.m.   Time to head home and tuck in early tonight.

Blackjack Road was dark and deserted. My headlights swept over the fields as I negotiated the sharp twists and turns. There were no street lights out here to dull the evening skies—or to light my way.

I scanned the sides of the road for the glint of deer eyes in the headlights.   There are an amazing number of deer in Illinois, about 800,000! 17,000 of those deer are in Jo Daviess County, and a good number of them seem to live along Blackjack. Bambi and her kin romp through the woods and fields by day and spend a good part of their nights in small groups, crossing from one side of the road to the other. They were probably looking for a soft, safe spot to spend the night, just like me.

Walking through the door, I checked the phone for messages. Sure enough, the red light was blinking. I hit the play button and the computer generated voice announced, in equally stressed syllables, that I had: "Two new mess-a-ges. First mes-sage: 'Karen, Mark. Been trying to reach you on your cell. Any news on Peter? Give me a call.' Dial Tone."

Shoot. I was supposed to call Mark after lunch and I'd forgotten to turn on my cell. I'd better call him back now. I checked Caller ID and saw that he'd called me from home.

The machine continued, "Se-cond mess-age play-back. 'Karen, this is Ken Kruse. Thought I'd see how you were and give you an update. Give me a call, 9999.' Dial tone."

The second message surprised me. I didn't expect the Coast Guard to give me personal updates. It was nice of him to call though. I decided to call Captain Kruse first. He might have news. The proverbial butterflies fluttered in my stomach as I dialed his number. He answered on the third ring.

"Captain Kruse, it's Karen Prince, returning your call."

"Karen, I'm glad you called." His deep voice resonated even through the phone lines. I pictured his clear blue eyes. "But please, call me Ken. I'm sure you're wondering about your friend, Peter. Unfortunately, we haven't found anything new yet. The *Lincoln* spent the day looking down river. They went as far as Lock and Dam 13 at Clinton. They checked out the islands along the way too." There was an awkward silence which he filled, saying, "But we'll keep looking for at least another 24 hours."

"What if you don't find him by then?"

There was another pause.

"If we don't find him by then, I'm afraid the odds of our finding him are pretty slim. I'd hoped that with daylight we'd spot him on one of the islands. But we've had boats past the entire area. We'll do the same thing tomorrow, just in case we missed him."

"I see," I said. The reality that Peter might be dead was sinking in. "Well, thanks for letting me know the situation." Neither of us rushed to say goodbye.

I broke the silence myself asking, "How's Baxter?" It seemed too trivial a question after Ken's report. But he answered, without missing a beat.

"He's fine. He's sleeping under the pool table right now. That's his den, I guess."

"The pool table? Sort of a funny choice for a den isn't it?"

"My desk and the TV are in the same room. Guess he likes to be with me. And he knows I can't trip over him when he's under there," he said with a hint of a laugh.

"Guess that's right."

"How was your day?" Ken asked.

"I went to the Museum—trying to keep things going for the exhibition until Peter's back." That generated a small pause in the conversation. "Cavanaugh was there. He went through their offices— Peter's and Lois's, I mean."

"Well, let's hope Peter turns up on one of those islands tomorrow," Ken said.

"Yes, let's hope so," I said. "Well, I just walked in the door. I guess I'd better get going."

"I'm sure you're exhausted after being up all last night. I'll talk to you tomorrow, as soon as there's some news."

"Thanks, I'd appreciate that," I said and hung up the phone.

His image lingered in my mind. I shook my head to clear it and dialed Mark's number. Mark must have been right next to the phone because it had barely rung when he answered.

"Karen, how are you?" He has Caller ID, as well. "And hey, I'm sorry I had to leave last night. I was wrapped up in meetings all day but I've been thinking about you."

I slumped into the overstuffed chair in front of the fireplace. It was comforting to hear Mark's voice. "No, no problem. I'm sorry I didn't call you back after lunch. It's been quite a day."

"I should have stayed last night."

"No, Mark. I realize you have your practice. And I know how that is," I said. I'd practiced law myself in Chicago for eight years before I'd left the city for my country life.

"I know you do. We couldn't do this otherwise, I'm sure," he said.

The "this" was our long distance relationship. I paused and pressed on, "I do miss your not being here though." There was silence. Neither of us wanted to get into an argument but neither of us could honestly say this long distance thing was really working. The fact that we saw each other so little lately made it even harder to address the issue. There always seemed to be something more important to talk about, and right now it was Peter and Lois.

Mark's mind must have been thinking along the same lines because instead of responding to my comment he simply said, "Have you heard anything about Peter?"

"Only that there's no news and that's not good. The Coast Guard's been searching all day. The *Mississippi Lady* did identify the life jacket. It was from the boat we were on last night. I assume it was the one Graziella tossed to Peter."

"How is she doing?" Mark asked.

"It's getting harder on her the longer this goes without any word," I said.

"I'm sure it is," he said.

I leaned back in my chair and took a deep breath. "I found some interesting things at the Museum today." I filled him in on the files on Lois's computer: her birth family; the sister who resented her showing up; the note to Peter about Evan; and the letter to Goth Gorski, the stalking boyfriend. I respected Mark's intellect and it was helpful to talk this through with him.

"Good heavens. You certainly have turned up a hornet's nest," Mark said.

"There's more," I said. "I was out at Graziella's—wait, did I tell you about the note I found from Lois?"

"Note? No you didn't, what note is that?"

"Well, let me start at the beginning. You know Lois was trying to talk to me on the boat yesterday, right?"

"Right—"

"Well, when I got to the Museum what do I find on my desk, but a note from Lois. Talk about creepy. It was like I could hear her voice when I read it."

"Well, what did the note say?"

"It said she'd found something in the old mine on Peter's property, and she wanted to talk to me about it."

"Did she say what she found?"

"No. She just said she'd found it the night before, in the old mine, and she didn't know who to tell about it, but that she figured I'd know what to do."

"So you think it's about the GAM?"

"That was my guess. That's the only thing Lois and I worked on together," I said.

"So, did you go look?" Mark asked.

"I did. I went to the mine when I was at Graziella's. And Mark, there were three paintings wrapped in a tarp, hidden in the mine!"

"Paintings? What kind of paintings?"

"Well, they're copies of three of the paintings in the exhibit!"

"You mean the exhibit at the GAM now?"

"Yes! At least I think they're copies. Mark, what if they're the originals? What if someone stole them and was hiding them in the mine?"

97

"What did you do with them?"

"I put them back," I said, somewhat sheepishly. As I said this out loud, it occurred to me that I should have taken them. What if they were the originals, and now they were gone? I could really have blown this!

Silence from Mark's end. Then he said, "Karen, I think you ought to call Cavanaugh and get out there with him now, before those things disappear."

I knew I needed to call Cavanaugh, but it hadn't seemed so urgent until now. "You know, you're right. I'll call him"

"Call him now, all right?"

"Yes, I will. I'll call you back."

"Talk to you in a minute then."

I dialed Detective Cavanaugh's home number. I didn't think he'd be at the sheriff's office at this time of night. And I was right. He picked up, sounding somewhat annoyed at the intrusion.

"Detective Cavanaugh, it's Karen Prince."

"Karen, how are you doing? I'm afraid I don't have any news for you about your friend—not as yet, at least."

"No, I heard that from Ken Kruse just a little bit ago."

There was a pause. Cavanaugh was probably wondering why I'd called him. I jumped in, "Detective Cavanaugh, I have some news. Well, not news exactly, but something I found— several things really." I took a deep breath. I hate it when I ramble like that. "Wait. Let me start from the beginning. You know the note I found from Lois?"

"You went to the mine!" It was a statement rather than a question.

I cringed, knowing he was thinking I should leave this sort of thing to him. "Yes, I did. I figured I'd just take a look since I was out there to check on Graziella anyway," I said.

"And what did you find?" he asked.

"Well, I found something really odd. I found three paintings—copies of three paintings from the exhibition," I said. "The thing is, I can't say for sure that they're the copies. I mean, what if they're the originals?"

There was silence, then he said, "I see what you mean. Did you ask Graziella if she knew anything about them? Maybe Peter stored them in the mine."

"No. Peter would never have put paintings in there. It's too damp. And Peter would know that. Paintings need a controlled temperature and humidity. That's why museums have special air control systems to keep the galleries at 50 percent humidity and between 65 and 70 degrees."

"So who do you think put those paintings there?"

"Well, I don't know, of course. But Evan is the one who rents the cabin right there. And he's Peter's apprentice, studying old master techniques. So he could have made the copies," I said.

"And what do you want me to do about this?"

"I hate to say this, but I think we'd better go get those paintings. What if they're the originals?"

"You're afraid someone might take them from the mine?"

"Yes, I am. Is there any way you could come out there with me tonight and get them?

"Karen, it's pitch black out there now. I don't know that we'd find our way to the mine, let alone into and through it. I'll tell you what. I'll meet you there first thing in the morning."

I hesitated. I wanted to go now, but I could see his point. "First thing?"

"Yes, I'll meet you at the Pierpoint residence at six a.m.," he said.

I exhaled heavily. "All right. I'll call Graziella and tell her."

There was another pause. "Don't do that. I'd suggest we not tell anyone about this until we have the paintings in hand."

I could see his point. We didn't know who'd put them there. I didn't think it was Graziella but there was no point in spreading the word about this. "So we'll just meet in her drive?" I asked.

"Yes. We'll walk to the mine from there," he said.

"I'll see you then."

"All right," Detective Cavanaugh said, and hung up.

Just as I put the receiver down, I remembered I'd forgotten to tell him about Goth's letters. I considered calling him back, but I really didn't want to face his annoyance with me again. I'd tell him tomorrow morning—first thing.

Chapter Eleven

Spelunking

I woke up just before five a.m. with Truffs curled between my ankles. She looked at me, shocked at this early morning wake up call, then rose and did one of those elongated cat yoga stretches. I jumped out of bed, into the shower, and into my clothes, in quick succession. Truffs was waiting for me in the kitchen when I made my way down there, preparing to leave. I opened her favorite can of Fancy Feast and set it down in front of her. She had me well trained.

Driving to Graziella's I thought about my plans for the day. Hopefully getting the paintings would go quickly and smoothly. I could head out from there and be in Madison in two hours. And I had to remember to tell Cavanaugh about the packet of Goth's letters. He may already have found them, but if he hadn't, he should see them. Sounded like a plan.

Just before six a.m., I pulled up to the barn and parked on the far side, out of sight from Graziella's. The house was still dark which was probably good. Dawn was just turning the sky a golden pink and I got out and looked at the dark underside of the clouds. Cavanaugh pulled up next to me a few minutes later, promptly at six. We were both in hiking boots and jeans with long sleeved jackets and hats. The woods in this county were notorious for their multiflora rose bushes and buckthorn trees, both of which seemed to reach out and tear at anything that came near. But forewarned is forearmed, and our four arms were duly covered.

"You lead the way," Cavanaugh said without preamble as he came up to me.

"We follow the trail for a ways through this field," I said, nodding towards the adjoining pasture. "Then we hike through the woods for about half a mile. Do you think we should leave any notes on our cars—in case Graziella's wondering who parked here, I mean?"

"I don't think that's necessary. She knows your car, doesn't she?"

I looked at the Boxster. It was pretty distinctive. "I guess she'd know it was me," I said and headed out on the trail I'd taken with the ATV yesterday afternoon. I took this chance to tell Cavanaugh about the packet of letters I'd found in Lois's office, as well as the two letters I'd retrieved from the Recycle Bin on Lois's computer. This led, as I knew it would, to a curt discussion of our respective roles. Neither of us held any illusions. Cavanaugh knew, based on past experience, that I wasn't likely to sit on the sidelines when my friends' lives were involved. And for my part, I knew he really couldn't make me a party to his investigation. So, we'd just have to leave it at that.

We started out on Peter's mowed trail and tromped in silence except for the sounds of our steps and the birds' morning songs. I listened to the wood thrushes' flute-like call: three rising notes answered by three descending ones. The cardinals' clear whistle stood out among the bird choir, as did the phoebes repeating their name: "fee-bee, fee-bee." I preferred to listen to the sounds of nature instead of man and, so it appeared, did Cavanaugh.

Five minutes later the path took a turn into the woods. Here the trail was lined with oak, hickory, eastern red cedar, and mulberry trees. The first two are hardwoods, and just starting to leaf out. The eastern red cedars keep their foliage all year. The mulberry trees are soft wood and grow so quickly their branches often break under their own weight.

But they do offer the sweetest of sweet berries from June through August. Mulberries are so fragile there's no way to eat them without staining your fingers, and often your clothes, purple with their juice. But they're definitely worth it.

The trail was mostly dirt and sparse grass now. Round lobed hepatica loved this wooded area, and clusters of lavender and white blossoms appeared on six inch stems, poking out among last year's fallen oak leaves. We passed two huge limestone rock outcroppings covered with pink and white Dutchman's breeches. These were among the first of the wildflowers. They have a delicate fern-like leaf that manages to grow from the smallest crevices on the face of the rocks. I spotted the first of the bloodroot as well. They're the queen of the spring wildflowers—two inches across, with eight glowing white petals and seemingly hundreds of deep golden yellow stamens surrounding a single pistil. The bloodroot flower emerges from the center of a whorled leaf. The leaf unfolds to form a perfect backdrop: six inches long, bluish-green, with pale veins and deeply scalloped lobes. Each of these wildflowers will show themselves for two weeks at most. Their ephemeral nature made them all the more exciting to see.

As we made our way lower into the valley, deer and turkey trails crossed our path. You could see their narrow, well worn trails across the wooded hillside. Suddenly, there was a huge crashing sound above us. I screamed involuntarily and covered my head as I crouched and looked up. Three turkeys flapped their way clumsily from their treetop roosts to the hillside behind us. My heart pounded out of all proportion to the cause, and I realized how tense I was about this morning's stealth adventure. Turkeys average 18 or 20 pounds and have a four foot wingspan. They spend their days on the ground, scratching the earth for insects and avoiding coyotes. They can fly if they need to, and they do sleep in trees. They're definitely not the most graceful of creatures when they're making their way in and out of their roosts, doing more thumping and thrashing among the tree branches than you'd think was good for them. These big birds had nearly vanished from this area 20 years ago, but they are now one of the true success stories of wildlife restoration.

Another ten minutes hike and we came to the stream at the base of the valley. This is where those hiking boots came in handy. The stream cut back and forth across the trail, and we had to scramble up and down the sides of the slippery three foot banks. Right now, the water was only a few inches deep, but it was running pretty well from the spring rains. Broken limestone rocks covered the layer of gray clay called shale that lined the stream bed. I bent to pick up one of the loose rocks and examined it. There were beak-like fossils embedded in every side. These were actually bivalves, the early ancestors of today's clams and mussels. I recognized these as the same fossils I'd found and identified from my own stream. They're from the Ordovician Period, 430 million to 500 million years ago. I'd also found Halysites and other corals on the upper ridge of my property, dating from the Silurian era, some 300 million to 400 million years ago. And still laying there today! I always find that mind boggling—how everything changes and still remains the same.

We passed the cabin but I didn't stop this time. Evan's car was there but no lights were on. I hoped we'd be in and out of the mine before he even woke up. I was leading the way, so I pointed to the cabin and put my finger to my lips in the age old children's sign for quiet. Cavanaugh nodded, and we stepped as quietly as we could through the woods around the cabin, down the path to the mine.

A few minutes later we were standing at the back of the shed housing the mine shaft. I looked down at the woodchuck hole then up at Cavanaugh. Uh-oh. There was no way he was going to fit through there. We walked around to the front and, unfortunately, the pad lock was still on the door. Cavanaugh looked at me expectantly.

"I went in through the hole," I whispered.

He furrowed his brows questioningly.

I nodded for him to follow me and went back to the woodchuck entryway.

"I'll go in and see if I can find a way to open the door," I whispered. Cavanaugh didn't seem to have a better plan, so I lay down, poked my head and shoulders through the jagged opening, and wiggled my way into the shed.

Inside, dawn's early light wasn't very bright. I'd come prepared, this time, with a flashlight. I grabbed it from my jacket pocket and walked the ten feet to the door, careful to avoid the open railed area in the center of the dirt floor. I scanned the door hinges and considered the possibility of removing them. They looked pretty well rusted in place. It occurred to me that I really needed to find a larger opening. Not just so Cavanaugh could join me in this bit of spelunking, but so we could get the paintings out of here. Well, if worse came to worse, I suppose I could enlarge the hole I'd just squirmed through.

I walked over to the lone window and ran the flashlight along the edge. Hey, this might just work! There were crude pegs holding in the wooden framed pane of glass. That window couldn't be very rain-proof, but it would be pretty easy to remove. I bammed the butt-end of the flashlight into each of the wooden pegs, then started pulling them out, one at a time. There were eight of them, and after the first four I realized I could have a problem as I got to the last ones.

I stuck my head out the woodchuck hole and whispered for Cavanaugh to come around to the window and help me. There was a handle on the exterior base of the window frame and Cavanaugh held that with one hand and braced the top of the frame with the other as I continued bamming and pulling pegs. Four more pegs and we had the thing out.

Cavanaugh leaned the frame against the side of the shed and climbed through the empty hole. I flashed my light on the rail guarded hole in the center of the floor. Cavanaugh gestured with his hand, in the classic "after you" motion. I started down.

Careful step after careful step, I descended into this chiseled passageway. I stopped five steps in and aimed my light up where the candles were on the side of the wall. We didn't need them, but I wanted Cavanaugh to get the full picture.

A few more steps and we were standing in the open area where the tunnels merged.

"They're in that one," I said pointing my light into the tunnel where I'd found the paintings. My heart raced at the sight of the empty space. Shoot! They weren't there! Then my light went back another foot and was reflected back to me off the tarp. Thank heavens!

I crouched, went into the tunnel, pulled the tarp off the paintings and handed it back to Cavanaugh. Then, one by one, I passed the three paintings out to him.

When I'd given him the last one, I made my way out and found Cavanaugh looking at the Ruysch.

"Incredible, isn't it?" I said.

"It is. And this is the copy you think?"

"Well, it could be," I said, and looked at the back of the canvas. Those stretcher bars sure looked old to me. "It could be the original. We'll have to examine it carefully and see," I said. "We might even need to do some x-rays or carbon dating."

"Really, I didn't know you did that with paintings. What would the x-rays tell you?"

"What the under painting is like. We'll compare it to the x-rays of other Ruysch paintings and see if the paint applications are consistent with her style."

"And I suppose the carbon dating will tell you the age of the paint?"

"Exactly. But a good forger would use period paint, so that might not be conclusive."

"How would they get paint from that time. You said these were from the 1700's."

"Forgers buy old paintings and scrape the paint off the canvasses, regrind it, and use it in their forgeries."

"Sounds like a lot of trouble."

"The prices these paintings bring make it worth their while. A Ruysch would go for $8 million at auction, easy."

"This flower painting, worth $8 million?" he asked, looking at it with renewed interest and a more appraising eye.

"If it's the original it would be. Of course, this wouldn't be being sold at open auction. Stolen goods, so it would bring the traditional ill-gotten gains discount. I'd guess someone would pay a million or two though."

"And what about these other two."

"Well, the two Heade's are from the late 1800's, and more of his works have survived. But American works are very collectible, so I'd say they'd bring about $2 million each at auction."

"So maybe they'd bring a million for the pair from a collector who wasn't interested in where they came from huh?

"About that, I'd say."

"Well, let's get these out of here."

"Right."

We retraced our steps, replaced the window, and made our way back to our cars.

"I ought to take these into evidence, but I don't want to be holding $12 million worth of paintings in the sheriff's office. How long would it take to do those tests you were talking about, so we know what we're dealing with here?"

"Well, I can do some initial studies at the Museum this morning. But I'll tell you what, I have a friend in the Art History Department at the University of Wisconsin. He does this kind of authentication for museums all around the country. If you'd like, I could ask him to take a look at these and, if he's there, we could have an answer in a day or so."

"I would like that. Give me his name and number, and I'll log these into evidence and out for expert examination. What kind of fees are we talking about? Am I going to need a special line item in the county budget for this?"

"I think he'll work with us," I said.

The Boxster has two trunks, one in the back and one under the hood, where the engines are in most cars. In the Boxster, the engine is behind the driver's seat—what they call a mid-car engine. You have to be a mechanic to access it, which accounts for the extraordinary cost of maintenance. But, I'm digressing again. The point is, even though the Boxster is a little car, I had plenty of room for the paintings. I put one in each of the two trunks with plenty of room to spare. I wrapped the third one in the tarp and placed it in the passenger's seat. Visions of the wind whisking that painting out of the car and sending it flying down the highway caused me to leave the top up on the Boxster. Oh well, too noisy on the highway anyway.

"I'll call my friend and head to Madison this morning," I said. "I'll stop at the Museum and get the other three paintings, just for comparison."

"Good. Let me know as soon as you learn something."

"I will."

This was fitting in nicely with my plan to find Goth Gorski today. Two birds with one trip.

Chapter Twelve

Mad Town

I wasn't in my typical travel attire, but hey, this was M-town, Mad Town, home of my alma mater. When I'd gone to school there, jeans were *de rigueur*. So I picked up the three paintings from the Museum and headed out right from there.

Tuesday traffic wasn't bad. The two lane blacktop road that was the major artery out of Galena wound through rolling hills and occasional small farm towns. This was my favorite part of country driving here: the quiet and the broad vistas as you crested a hill. I passed a pasture filled with shiny Black Angus. Yes, I know they're beef cattle, but I prefer to think of the peaceful lives they'll have this summer. Just another reminder to enjoy what we have now. In fact all we really have is now.

I stayed on meandering country roads and avoided the major highway to Madison. Rolling fields extended as far as the eye could see. These fields were not flat like Nebraska's, but more rolling like the Tuscan countryside. You see, our little part of the world was uniquely spared from the great leveling effects of the glaciers. For some reason, not once, but at least twice, the glaciers coming down from the north actually parted, went around our area, and rejoined south of here. That is why we have these beautiful rolling hills while most of the Midwest is unrelentingly flat.

Small burgs of 200 to 800 people appeared along the way. They were probably formed around the grain elevators and stage coach stops when the land was first tilled. The soybeans' new green shoots followed the contours of the hills emphasizing the swales and rises. Trees fringed the perimeters of the fields and formed a puzzle pattern of receding rectangles. Normally, on this sort of drive my mind would wander to that thought-free meditative state, but today, ideas flitted across my mind about Peter, Lois, Evan, paintings and mineshafts. At nine a.m. I called Arthur Doyle on my cell and let him know I had a special project for him. Happily, he was in town, didn't have a morning class and agreed to look at my paintings right away. We arranged to meet at the Elvehjem, the University's 30 year old art museum. With its grey cement walls formed into oversized smooth blocks, it had been one of the newer buildings on campus when we were students. Now, Arthur had his office in the adjoining classroom building and, as the Museum's Historian, he had access to the locked, air controlled museum painting storage facility. He'd agreed to store the six paintings there while he performed his analysis.

I pulled into the reserved parking spaces, (nice to have friends in high places) and Arthur met me at the side door. We'd gone to undergrad together here and spent many hours in this very museum. I remembered our meeting that first day in Art History 101. We'd had a sort of contest, raising our hands to be the first to identify the slides Professor Longo flashed on the screen in the huge auditorium. Of the 300 students in that freshman art history class, the two of us became life long friends. I couldn't tell you the name of a single other student. It's funny how that happens. We met, we clicked, and I knew we'd be friends for life. And here I was, over 20 years later, looking for Arthur's help. Well, if anyone could determine the authenticity and attribution of these paintings, it was Arthur. I'd trust his results any day.

Arthur was tall, thin and groomed to perfection. Even in this wash and wear era, his shirts and pants were meticulously pressed. We carried the paintings into the locked storage area ourselves, and Arthur gave me a written receipt. He said he would fax a copy to Detective Cavanaugh as well.

"Thanks, Arthur. That'd be great. When do you think you'll be able to tell us which paintings are the originals and which are the copies?"

"Well, I'd say I'd have an answer for you within the week. Maybe as soon as tomorrow, but I don't want to promise that. Luckily, here at the university, I have access to the equipment I need. Otherwise it would take months to send the paint scrapings and canvas clippings away to a laboratory and wait for the results."

"Great. Well, I'll be in this area the whole day. I have to go to Rainbow to find someone. I'll give you a call before I leave in case there's anything else you need."

"I'll call you on your cell if anything comes up before then."

"Thanks, Arthur," I said, gave him a hug and headed out to find the mysterious Goth Gorski.

Rainbow was a small town, taken over by hippies in the 70's. Its original name was changed by majority vote of the community after the hippies got involved in running the town. Who says politics and hippie-dom don't mix? Anyway, it's been a minor tourist attraction since the houses there began to rival the Painted Ladies of San Francisco. What the Rainbow houses lack in bric-a-brac detail, they make up for in wild intense colors. I hadn't been there in years, and I wondered how much it would have changed.

It took about 25 minutes of driving to get to Rainbow. I used the time to review what I knew about Goth Gorski and to consider my approach. It seemed clear that he was obsessed with Lois. His showing up at events at the GAM combined with the barrage of letters amounted to stalking. Yes, it's true that the GAM events are open to the public, and that he and Lois had been in art classes together at the UW. But Goth had access to innumerable art shows in Madison,

Milwaukee, and Chicago. I figured it was Lois and not our local art events that drew him to the GAM.

I'd done a Map Quest search for his address: 750 Main. I assumed that wouldn't be too hard to find, and I was right. Highway FF which led into town conveniently turned into Main Street. Suddenly, it was as if someone had turned the color adjusters up on a TV screen. Red, blue, orange, green and yellow houses lined the street. Small stores featured organic food and tie dyed clothing.

I caught an address, 850. Getting close. On the next block I spotted a yellow house with purple shutters, and the numbers 75 and a stain where the zero had once been. This was it.

I pulled into the drive and saw an old school bus, painted the same purple as the shutters, parked behind the house. I got out and walked up the cracked sidewalk. The "lawn" would have made a prairie restorationist's heart leap for joy. Looked like it hadn't been touched in years.

There was a patch of duct tape over a bump to the right of the door. Hmm. Guess the door bell wasn't working. I opened the storm door and knocked on the small glass window in the center of the wooden door. I shaded my eyes and looked in, listening for movement. Good grief! The foyer was purple. Must have been a great sale on that color. But no signs of life. I tried the door knob. By gosh, the handle turned and I felt the latch pull back. Decisions, decisions. I gave the door a little push and peeked inside.

"Hello. Anyone home?"

Silence.

"I'm looking for Goth Gorski. Is he here?"

There was a rustling sound from somewhere inside the house. I pulled my head back and stood properly on the stoop. Listening intently, I heard footsteps approach as I pulled the door closed.

A shaggy dark haired young man re-opened the door. He was in a tie-dyed, what else—purple, t-shirt and torn jeans. He wore leather sandals on his feet and a piece of knotted black leather around his neck. He had three pierced parts that I could see. There were probably more, but I didn't want to think about that.

"Are you Goth Gorski, by any chance?" I asked as nicely as I could.

"Who's asking?"

"I'm Karen Prince, a friend of Lois Fretmeyer."

That seemed to get his attention and he opened the door wider.

"She send you here?" he asked with a confused look.

"Not exactly. I want to talk to you about her is all. Can I come in for a minute?"

He hesitated, looked me over, and then said, "All right."

I followed him into the living room, but it was more like following him into a cave. The walls were black as was the sparse furniture. There was a sofa, a few chairs, and a coffee table. The edges of the walls and the furniture seemed to be painted in a silver paint. When he switched on the overhead light, I saw why. They glowed under the black light, an eerie purplish white color. There were shades over the windows keeping out any natural light. Intricate geometric patterns in day-glow colors appeared on the walls under the black light. He smiled as I stared at the designs.

"Nice, huh?" he asked.

"Incredible," was all I managed to say.

"I did it."

I tensed and looked at him.

"You did it?" I hadn't expected a confession and found myself edging toward the door. Don't killers usually say that right before they shoot the person?

"The walls. I painted the walls. That's what I do. For night clubs and stuff, you know."

"Oh." I started breathing again. "Nice."

"So, why do you want to talk to me about Lois?"

"Ah, Goth, were you by any chance on the cruise on Sunday?"

"Cruise? What cruise are you talking about?"

"The one Lois was on, Sunday, on the Mississippi." He was lying. Either he didn't know that Dara saw him by the boat on Sunday, or he knew but figured his best chance was to deny being there anyway.

"No, I haven't seen Lois in weeks, not since the last GAM exhibit."

"Have you spoken to her?"

"What are all the questions about?" He seemed suddenly angry. He clenched and unclenched his fists repeatedly and glared at me.

"I thought you might have heard. Why don't you sit down a minute."

"What? What are you talking about?" The fists continued.

I found myself charting a getaway in case this fellow went crazy on me, and then said: "Lois passed away on Sunday."

"What? Passed away? You mean she's—she's dead?"

"Yes, I'm afraid she is."

Now he sat down.

"How?"

"Drowned. She went overboard—off the boat."

"Are you sure?"

"Very."

"Why did you come here to tell me?"

"We're not sure it was an accident." I watched his face. There was nothing subtle about his response.

114

"What! Are you telling me someone pushed her? Someone drowned her? I'll kill them! I'll kill them myself!"

Was this all an act? Or maybe he had one of those split personalities you hear about. Suddenly he was crying. Huge howling sobs. This was getting scary.

"I'm sorry to bring you this terrible news. I know you cared for Lois very much."

He stopped suddenly and glared at me. In an angry voice he said, "I loved her. I admit it. I always loved her. From the day we met in drawing class." Then he covered his face and started crying again. He seemed lost in his grief.

"Excuse me a minute," I said. "I'll just use your ladies room and leave you alone."

He made no indication of hearing me, and I went through the only doorway connecting the living room to the rest of the house. It was a small house. Left led to the kitchen. Right, down the hallway, must lead to the bathroom and the bedrooms. I could see two doorways just ten feet apart. The first was the bathroom, which I didn't go into. The second was a bedroom, converted into a studio of sorts. Paint cans were stacked against one wall. A drawing table covered with papers was in one corner. The far wall, oh! The far wall was covered in photos and drawings—of Lois. Ick! I'd seen things like that in TV stories. It was much scarier in real life. I backed out of the room. The hallway took a right turn, and, even if I shouldn't have, I followed it. Five more paces and the hall ended in a second bedroom. This one was his bedroom. It was a mess. The kind you'd expect from a 13 year old: clothes everywhere, the bed unmade. There was a computer on the desk in the corner. I took it all in quickly and headed back to the living room. Goth was still sitting on the sofa with his head in his hands when I returned. I don't think he'd even noticed I'd left.

"I'm going now. Is there someone you want me to call. Someone to keep you company?"

He shook his head no.

"Are you sure you'll be all right if I leave?"

He looked up this time. He seemed clear for the moment. "I'll be all right. Just let me know who did this."

"Of course," I said, and let myself out the door.

Well, that was certainly weird. But was he weird enough to kill Lois? I suppose he'd had enough mood swings in those ten minutes to make me wonder.

I climbed into the Boxster and drove to the outskirts of Rainbow. I gave Arthur a call but got his answering machine. I left a message telling him I'd decided to head back and asked him to give me a call as soon as he had any news. It was still early enough that I figured I could drive by Lois's birth family's farm on my way home.

Chapter Thirteen

Bully for Ewe

It was just after noon when I left Rainbow. By two I was slowing down as I came into Scales Mound. I had the address for the Woods' farm and found it using my trusty county road map. The Boxster handled these back roads just fine. They were all seal coated and fairly well maintained. It was usually the driveways that gave me a problem. Between the steep hills and the rain erosion, I had to take it really slow to avoid getting the bottom of the Boxster hung up as I made my way up to the farm house.

The driveway was a full half mile long and twisted and turned its way up to the top of a 200 foot hill. Red Angus grazed the pasture on both sides of the drive. There was a herd of llamas to my left in a separate fenced in area. Llamas were becoming an almost common sight out here as hobby farmers added these once exotic creatures to their critter collections. I hadn't called ahead, but I hoped on a Tuesday afternoon my chances would be pretty good for finding someone from the family at home running the business. And I was right.

A lanky fellow in his mid-20's was leading a gorgeous black horse from the paddock into the barn. The horse whinnied as I pulled up to the white two story farm house 30 feet away from the barn.

"Hello," I said, walking directly up to him.

"Good afternoon. Can I help you?"

"Yes. I hope so anyway. I was looking for Mary Wood." I figured I'd start with Lois's mother.

"That's my mother. She's not seeing anyone right now though. Maybe I can help you. I'm Fred Wood."

I wondered if she'd heard the news about Lois or if she was just not feeling well given her ongoing battle with cancer. Could be both I suppose.

"Thanks, Fred. Maybe you can. I'm Karen Prince. I'm with the Galena Art Museum and I was a friend of Lois Fretmeyer."

"Oh, I see. Yes, we heard the news. The sheriff called yesterday morning. Mom's taking it pretty hard."

"I'm so sorry."

"Thanks. We'd all just reconnected, you see. And it's been a shock, just finding each other and now, losing her so quickly. But, if you know Lois, I guess you know all about that."

"Some. Maybe you can fill me in on the parts I don't know." A small pug came running up to us from the stable. He leaped around our ankles, anxious to say hello.

"Winston, sit. Good boy." The dog paid little attention to Fred's command, and I guess I wasn't encouraging discipline because I stooped down and gave Winston a rub, which sent his tail wagging even faster. The horse whinnied in annoyance at being kept from his stall.

"Just a minute. Let me put Shadow in the stable and I'll be right with you. You can come along if you'd like."

"Sure," I said, rising and following him into the stable. Winston came too, running in circles around me and giving little barks of delight at having company. The stable was new, with stalls for 30 horses. It looked like less than half of them were occupied at the moment. This was no ordinary country stable. There were ceiling fans and carved plaques with each animal's name above its stall. The floor was cleanly swept and various tacks and saddles hung outside several of the stalls. "Nice place," I said.

"Thanks, we built it a few years ago. We use this as our breeding center."

I must have had a quizzical look on my face because he smiled and said, "Bully for Ewe. That's our family's business, breeding animals."

"Right, right. Bully for Ewe. So you run the business?"

"I do, along with my brother, Carter."

Just then we heard a horse approach at a gallop and come to a sudden stop outside the stable.

"Whoa, Nellie, Whoa!"

I turned to see Fred's double riding up to us on a chestnut mare and pulling sharply on the reigns. The horse stomped the ground in protest at the sudden stop. Actually, I don't know much about horses and tend to anthropomorphize. I assume an animal is thinking whatever I'd be thinking if I were them. Anyway, Fred's double dismounted, led the mare into the first stall, then joined Fred and me.

"Karen, this is my brother, Carter. Carter, Karen Prince."

I extended my hand to him. Carter met the gesture with a strong shake and a stiff smile. I got the feeling he didn't like strangers.

"Guess you two are twins," I said.

"What gave it away?" Fred said with an easy laugh. So much for the time of birth setting your personality. These twins' personalities were obviously very different.

"Karen here wants to talk to us about Lois," Fred said. "How about we take a minute and go into the office?"

Carter nodded his assent and I followed the two of them into a room at the far end of the stable. The room was furnished with two desks and a small conference table ringed with chairs. The walls were covered with photos of what I assume were prized stallions and bulls. File cabinets were clustered in the far corner. Two large windows provided a view of the paddock.

"Have a seat," Fred said, pulling out a chair for himself. Carter walked around the table and sat opposite Fred. I took the seat at the head of the table so I could watch both of their expressions as we talked.

"Thanks." I wasn't quite sure how to start so I just jumped right in. "Can I ask you when you first found out that Lois was your sister?"

"Well, it was about three months ago I'd say. Mom had a call first, I think, from the Sisters of Charity. They handled the adoption you know. And I guess Lois must have gone to them and they called Mom. Then she came out here, Lois, I mean, and met with Mom and Dad. We didn't know anything about it until afterward. Mom and Dad told us about it one Sunday at dinner. The next Sunday after that she came over so we could all meet."

"How did you all get along?"

"It was weird. It was like we knew each other already. At least I felt that way. I don't think Rene liked her though. I think maybe because she was another daughter. I don't know. But they didn't seem to get along much," Fred said.

"What about you Carter? What did you think of Lois?"

"What was there to think? There wasn't any question about who she was. The Sisters guaranteed it was her. They kept track, I guess. And Mom and Dad didn't deny it. They admitted it."

"Admitted it?" He made it sound like a confession.

"Well, you don't think of your parents going around having children out of wedlock, do you? Giving up your sister for adoption! And all the lectures they gave us growing up!" He ended with a snort.

"Mom invited her to Sunday dinners from then on," Fred said.

"So you got together every week?"

"Yup, the whole family, every Sunday, Mom and Dad, kids, and grandkids," Fred said.

"Are either of you married?" I asked.

"I am," Fred replied. "Married two years, now. We've got one son, Little Fred."

I smiled, then looked at Carter. He shook his head, "Not me."

"What about your sister? Rene, is it?" I asked Fred.

"Yup, Rene's married. Two kids. Husband's gone though. Left just after the twins were born."

"Do you all live here on the farm?"

"No, we all have our own places. Bess and I bought the adjoining farm when we got married. Rene's got a place about five miles from here. And Carter here's got the acreage across the road," Fred said.

"Does this family business support all four families then?" I asked.

"Well, in a way, I guess you could say that," Fred said. "But it's really the Eclone stock that's paying today. This business does well, but the Eclone, that's just really taken off."

"What's Eclone?"

"Well, in 1995, Rene was in college at UW studying that cloning business. Carter and I, we went there through Ag school, but she went into bio-science. She graduated that year and started a company with two of her classmates. Well, she got us all to buy stock in that company and sure enough if they didn't come up with a new twist on cloning. Two years later they sold out to this California bio-tech company, Eclone, for mostly stock. They wanted whatever it was Rene had come up with. And then Eclone really hit the sky. We let Rene handle all that, but she says they're doing great with no signs of stopping. Carter and I, we do our breeding the old fashioned way," Fred said, with a laugh.

"So Rene handles the family's stock in Eclone?"

"Well, it's not really family stock. We all own our own stock, but she watches it for us all."

"Your Mom and Dad have the stock too?"

"Yup, they have the most actually. They were the ones who could afford to back Rene and her friends. But Mom and Dad have told us they plan to keep it all in the family. They've been talking about setting up a trust for us and our kids. Especially now with Mom being so sick."

"And what about Lois? Would she have been in that trust?"

Fred and Carter looked at each other, but neither spoke.

"I don't mean to pry into your family affairs, but I assume the sheriff told you we don't know how this happened. How Lois fell off the boat I mean."

"He told us," Fred said. There was a pause before he continued. "I don't know what Mom and Dad would have done about Lois. We'd talked about it, and I think they were going to make a provision for her. Everybody didn't agree on how that should be done though, you see."

"Who didn't agree?" I knew I was pushing him, but figured it was now or never.

"Well, you know, she wasn't a part of the family when we were growing up and when this whole cloning thing happened. Rene felt it was hers and her kids, and those of us who'd been there to help support her early on."

"And your Mom and Dad felt differently?" I ventured a guess. "Your folks wanted to provide something for all their children?"

"Yea, pretty much that's what it comes down to—or came down to. I guess it won't matter now," Fred said.

There was pause. "Do you think your Mom and Dad would be up to talking to me for a few minutes?" I asked.

"I'm sure they would. They want to do anything they can to help get to the bottom of what happened to Lois," Fred said. Carter remained silent even as we all rose to go to the house and find their parents.

"Mom will be on the screened-in porch. She spends most of her day there now. Sort of hard for her to get around so she likes to sit there. She can look out, feel the breeze, and we've got it set up so she can watch TV out there if she wants. Dad will probably be in his workshop. He's been busy making bluebird houses."

We walked the short distance to the house and found Mrs. Wood wrapped in an afghan, lying on the couch with a cat curled next to her. She moved to prop herself up as we entered her world.

"Mom, I brought you company. This is Karen Prince. She's here to talk to you about Lois. She's a friend of Lois's and is trying to find out how Lois came to fall off that boat." It was Fred again that did the talking, with his brother silently shadowing us.

I pulled a wicker chair closer to the sofa and sat down next to Mrs. Wood. She fussed a bit and got herself propped up enough that we were almost at eye level. "It's nice to meet you Mrs. Wood. I'm sorry about the circumstances. It must be awfully hard for you to have lost Lois so suddenly."

"Lots of hard things these days. We just go on as long as we can, as best we can."

"Yes, I guess we do. You know, I worked with Lois at the Museum. She was a wonderful young woman, Mrs. Wood. And I want to find out what happened to her."

"The police were here yesterday. They said she fell off the boat. Just like that—fell off the boat." Her voice drifted off and she turned away.

"I'm so sorry," I said. I looked at Fred who'd taken a chair at the table. Carter was sitting across from him.

"It's the morphine," Fred said. "Makes her come and go."

"I see." I wasn't going to learn much here. "Sorry to bother you, Mrs. Wood. And I'm so sorry for your loss."

I rose, and the two brothers followed me from the screened porch into the kitchen.

"She's better some times than others," Fred said. "You can try talking to her another time, but I don't know what she'd be able to tell you that might help."

"Yes, I see. I'm sorry. I didn't realize she was so ill."

"It's gotten much worse in the last few weeks. But you wanted to see Dad too, didn't you? I hear him working."

The buzz of an electric saw came from below us. We went through a door at the far end of the kitchen and down a steep set of stairs to the basement. The sawing sound got louder as we descended.

The basement turned out to be one room, about 30 by 40 feet, carved directly out of limestone. There were no windows and the air was damp and heavy. The floor was fairly new cement, which had probably been poured over the original earth floor.

Mr. Wood stood over a table saw with a foot long board in his hand. Dozens of bluebird houses sat on wooden shelves lining the wall behind him. He looked up at the three of us and turned off the saw. As the blade's buzzing slowed, Fred introduced me.

"Dad, Ms. Prince here wants to talk to you a bit, about Lois. How about we go upstairs and have a cup of coffee?"

"All right," he said curtly, apparently not pleased by the interruption.

The four of us marched back upstairs to the kitchen. I didn't think Mr. Wood was going to be very communicative, and it wasn't going to help to have his two sons observing the interview. Or maybe that would prevent him from just telling me to buzz off which is what his body language was saying.

Mr. Wood, Carter and I took seats around the big oak kitchen table while Fred put on a pot of coffee.

"Mr. Wood, I'm a friend of Lois's and I want to find out how she fell off that boat on Sunday."

"How do you think I'm going to help you with that?"

"Well, I understand Lois had just recently come into your family. I was wondering if when you were talking, she mentioned anything that was bothering her. Was there anyone she was afraid of, or who she had some trouble with?"

"Now, Ms. Prince,"

"Karen," I interrupted. "Please, call me Karen."

"Karen, I don't know how much you know about our family here. But Lois, she was lost to us for a long time. We lost her, and she found us, by the grace of God. And now she's gone again. We didn't have too much time together and though I loved her as a daughter, I can't say I knew too much about her, you see."

This was clearly a difficult subject for him. And I expect he was right. What would he know about Lois's life? If she was really troubled about something, it was more likely that she'd have confided in the parents that raised her than the family she was just getting to know.

"Yes, I see. I'm sorry to trouble you."

Just then, a tall thin woman in jeans and a black form fitting turtleneck entered the kitchen from the interior of the house.

"Hi, what's going on?" she said to the room in general.

Fred answered. "Rene, this is Karen Prince. She's a friend of Lois's."

Rene stopped where she was and said, "What do you want?"

125

Well, nice meeting you too, I thought, but said, "I'd like to know anything that will help figure out what happened to Lois on Sunday."

"The sheriff already told us. She fell off a boat and I'm afraid that's all there is to it."

"Maybe, but maybe not," I said, meeting her stare.

"What's the not?"

"Well, she may have been pushed overboard. As a matter of fact, that seems more likely to me than that she fell off the boat."

"Really. Who'd do that?"

"That's exactly what I intend to find out."

"Hmm. Well, I have no idea. And I don't see how we can help you. We really didn't know her very well. Even though we were actually sisters, we only met a few months ago. Freddie, did you tell her all that?"

"She knows the family history, Rene," Fred replied curtly. "She's only trying to help. So quit being such a—he paused. Just quit it."

Hmm, seemed these siblings didn't see eye to eye on Lois.

"Did you resent Lois's coming into your family?" I asked Rene.

She tilted her head and scrunched up her mouth. "You get right to the point. I like that. Well, I didn't buy the one big happy family thing she was trying to create. Her showing up here was hard on Mom, and on everyone. You don't just become a family all at once. It takes growing up together and making a home together that makes family. I don't know why she had to come here."

Her pointless anger moved me to pity. I saw Rene as a confused young woman, who was losing her mother to cancer. She probably unconsciously resented Lois's intrusion on their remaining time. I answered her in a quite voice, "Yes, I agree, shared experiences can bring people closer together. But you know, you could have started building memories with Lois as well and expanded your family." It really already was expanded, I thought. You just weren't aware of the fact until Lois found you. It's amazing how much energy is wasted in denial, trying to cling to the past.

"Well, it's all irrelevant now, isn't it?" Rene said. "Some things are just not meant to be. And she was not meant to be a part of our family."

"Don't you think you're being a bit harsh?" I asked as gently as I could. It saddened me to see someone so young being so closed.

But Rene had already turned and left the room before I finished my sentence.

"You have to excuse Rene. She's always been sort of eccentric. Smart about some things, like business and investing, but never did learn how to be with people," Fred said.

"Well, I won't take up anymore of your time. Sorry for the intrusion. If you think of anything you want to tell me, I'll leave my cell number for you."

And with that, I said my goodbyes and headed back home. If I hurried I could get there and check in with Detective Cavanaugh before he left for the day.

Chapter Fourteen

Touching Base

Driving home, I got out my cell phone and called Cavanaugh. Wow, I actually caught him in his office for once.

"Detective Cavanaugh, it's Karen Prince. I just thought I'd touch base with you. Any news from the Coast Guard?"

"No, nothing about Peter I'm afraid. But I do want to see you. Mind if I come over?"

"Ah, no, of course not, but I'm just headed home now. I should be there in about 20 minutes. How about meeting me there in 30? Will that work for you?" I asked, knowing it would take him almost that long to get to my place from his office.

"That'll be fine. I have a few photos I'd like to show you."

"Photos? From Sunday's boat trip?" I asked, wondering what he could have.

"No, this is something from Evan's cabin. I've got some photos of paintings I'd like you to see if you can identify for me."

Shoot, I thought. He's gone and searched the cabin without me! But I just said, "Well, sure. I'd be glad to take a look at them for you."

Then couldn't help but ask, "So did you get a search warrant or did Evan let you search the place without one?"

"I didn't give him the opportunity to decline. I called Judge Escher as soon as we left the mine. I had the warrant and was out there again by ten this morning."

"Excellent. I'll look at the photos and see what you've got. In fact, I'll call Arthur on my way home and maybe I'll have some information for you on the paintings too."

"See you in 30 minutes then," he said and hung up.

Arthur answered his cell phone on the first ring. "Arthur, it's Karen. Any news?"

"Didn't you get my message? I've been trying to reach you for the last hour!"

"No, I didn't. But if you left the message on my cell, it can take hours for the message to hit my voice mail. But anyway, you've got me now. So what's your verdict?"

"First, let me ask you, are you sure you had these labeled correctly? I mean, is there any chance you could have confused the paintings from the Museum with the ones from the mine?"

"Holy Moly! You mean the paintings in the mine were the originals! Oh my heavens! Oh, thank goodness we found them!"

"No kidding! These forgeries are really very good. Better than very good. Someone went through a lot of trouble to make these. They not only used the right materials, they got the artists' styles down pat. If it hadn't been for the ghost of the underlying images they tried to remove from the canvas they used, they might have stumped me. It's the best copying job I've ever seen!"

"Forgery job, you mean. If they hadn't put the duplicates in the Museum you might call it copying, but they were definitely trying to pass these off as the originals, so forgery would be the term to use," I said, then gasped as I gave the wheel a sharp yank to the right and skidded onto Sawmill. I'd nearly missed my turn in all the excitement.

"What do you want me to do with the paintings now?"

"Keep them under lock and key. I'm meeting with Detective Cavanaugh in ten minutes, and I'll have him give you a call with instructions. I'm sure they're "Exhibit A" now. You know about chain of custody don't you? Put them in a secure, locked place, where no one else has access to them, all right? Can you do that?"

"Sure, I can put them in one of the locked Elvehjem storage areas, and I'll use a separate locked bin. I'll send my assistant out for a padlock right now and I'll keep both keys."

"Thanks, Arthur."

"Don't worry about the paintings. Drive safely and call me when you've got the detective there. I'll wait here with the paintings until I hear from you." And with that he rang off.

Five minutes later, I was home. Truffs was particularly vocal in her greeting, probably due to my prolonged absence the past few days.

"Hey there," I said, trying to make my way into the kitchen with her weaving around my ankles. There was no way I was going to make forward progress until Ms. Truffs had been properly rubbed and fed. She had her priorities and I guess I obeyed. I scooped her up into my arms and stroked her silky black fur. She wasn't going to purr for a few minutes just on principle, I could see, but she leaned into my fingers, so I knew she wasn't too awfully put out. "Here," I said, shifting her into one arm and opening the cabinet that held her cat food with the other. I managed to open the can and tap the contents onto her dinner plate.

I hate to admit it, but I'd bought Truffs her own set of plates. Well, she didn't have the full set, just the bread size plates, or in this case, the cat food size. A potter friend of mine made them for us. They're a beautiful shade of pale pink, with very realistically painted pictures of mice on them. Truffs is a hunter and, I don't know for sure, but I like to think she enjoys the images of the mice. Anyway, it was my treat to her after I won the lottery a few years ago.

Truffs hopped happily out of my arms and sniffed her plate carefully before taking a tentative bite. Yup, the same food she'd been having for the past two years. But a cat can never be too careful, I guess.

I left her to her dinner and checked the machine. The red light was flashing. I hit the message playback button and stretched my stiff back as I listened to Ken Kruse's deep voice fill the room. I stopped stretching and listened. "Karen, just wondering how you were doing. No news on this front. I thought you might like some company though for dinner tonight. I could pick something up or we can go out. Give me a call." There was a bark from Baxter in the background, and then the dial tone.

Dinner? Really? I hadn't been asked out to dinner by a fellow other than Mark in several years. Well, it wasn't really a date, he was probably just lonely and looking for company. But, I supposed that is a date. I plopped myself down in my big overstuffed chair. No, this is just two people exploring a possible new friendship, I told myself. Boy, I didn't need this sort of complication.

The next message was from Mark. "Karen, just checking in. Any news? Give me a call at the office."

I opened the cabinet under the phone. A bottle of single malt Macallan's stood next to a box of handmade Galena chocolates. I retrieved two foil wrapped dark chocolates and replayed the messages as I ate them. Then I called Mark. I got his machine, as usual, and told him I was home, had no news, and to call me when he was free.

Then I called Ken. He was home.

"Ah, hi. It's Karen. Just returning your call."

"How are you doing? I wish I had better news for you, but so far we haven't found much. And I think they'll pretty much call us off the search by the end of the day."

"Hmm." I found myself a bit tongue-tied, probably because I wasn't sure what in the world I was going to say to him about his dinner proposal."

"Anything new at the Museum? About Peter, I mean?"

Boy, was there, but I didn't think I should share that with anyone until I'd talked to Cavanaugh. I hadn't felt so self conscious with anyone since I was a teenager. How awkward! I wondered why I'd called back.

"Hmm, nothing I can really talk about. I just wanted to return your call. Detective Cavanaugh is on his way over here now, and I'm not sure how long we'll be."

"Well, how about if I come over and bring something from the Gourmet Kitchen. You'll need to have some dinner and surely he'd be gone in a couple hours. I won't stay long. I need to run Baxter over to the vet for his annual exam and that's just a few miles from you. How about if I stop by at seven?"

I heard myself say, "Sure. That'd be nice." Then I panicked and added, "But I don't think I'll be up for dinner. It's just been too hectic to even think about eating."

"Well, you have to eat something. I'll just bring you a salad."

"Oh, all right. That'd be nice. Thanks." I hung up the phone and ate two more chocolates. Oh boy.

I dashed upstairs, washed my face and ran a brush through my hair. Cavanaugh would be here any minute. I moved to my closet and, thinking of my dinner date, changed into my most slimming pair of black pants and a white hand-knit turtleneck. I put on my new black Nikes and headed downstairs just as the doorbell rang.

"Detective Cavanaugh, come in. And thank you for coming here instead of asking me to come down to the station," I said, closing the door behind him and leading us into the living room. Cavanaugh selected a seat on the sofa, and I sat down across from him.

"This is what I need your help with," he said, opening a large brown envelope and pulling out photos of several paintings. I could see they were floral still life paintings as he pulled them from the envelope. As he handed them to me, I could see they were my floral still life paintings! I mean, paintings I had created! In fact, the third one was *"Butterfly Bouquet."* That very same painting that had turned up at auction in London last fall and been purchased by the Morgans. The thing was, my signature had been carefully painted over, and the painting placed in a 17th century Dutch frame, and passed off as a painting by one of the Dutch Masters. This was incredible! But that's another whole story.

The next photo was of Evan holding "Butterfly Bouquet" in the very same period Dutch frame.

"Good heavens," I gasped. "I certainly can identify this painting! I painted it! And, I can tell you it was sold at auction last fall to clients of Marshall Otillier, my gallery in New York. I identified it for them back then. And you say you found these photos in Evan's cabin?"

"Yes, they were in a locked box in his bedroom."

"Well, this explains a lot. The young man who sold this painting to the London auctioneers said it had been in his family in Amsterdam for generations. Of course, it couldn't have been. This ties it all together! I wondered how one of my works turned up there. Now we know!"

"And," I continued, "Arthur tells me that the three paintings we took from the mine this morning were the originals and the ones at the GAM were copies! I asked him to keep them labeled and under lock and key until he talks to you."

"Sounds like we have ourselves an art forger here."

"I'd say so! Where is he now?"

"One of my men is watching him. We haven't picked him up yet, but he won't get away."

I sank back into my chair as I absorbed this new information. Evan was an art forger. Was he also a murderer?

"Do you think Evan was the one who pushed Lois and Peter off the boat then?" I asked.

"I don't know yet, and I don't like to guess. With what you've told me now, I'll have my man bring him in to the station, and we'll see what he tells us."

"What about Goth?" I asked. "Dara told me she saw him hanging around the boat on Sunday."

"Yes, she told me too. And don't you go looking for that character, Karen. I checked with the Dane County Sheriff's Department and Goth Gorski has a record—for assault and battery. So stay away from him, you hear?"

"I hear you," I said. "Now he tells me!" I thought and quickly changed the subject. "Oh, before I forget, let me write out Arthur's number for you. He's waiting for your instructions on the paintings."

Then it struck me. We had the show opening at the GAM with three empty spaces on the wall. "Oh, good heavens! Detective Cavanaugh, do you think there's some way we could get the three originals back to the GAM for the reception Friday night?"

"I think we can arrange that. I'll have one of my men go to Madison to get the paintings. If you can have someone meet my man at the Museum tomorrow and have the paintings installed securely to the wall, I think we can let them be part of the exhibit."

"Thank you!" I didn't want to have to explain to everyone why three of the most important paintings in the exhibit were missing.

"I have a few more things I'd like you to look at for me," Cavanaugh said as he handed me a notebook.

I opened the book and found a list of some 20 paintings followed by names and addresses. I ran my finger down the list and stopped at the names of the three paintings that had been taken from the GAM. Across from each of these paintings was the name: Henry Heckle. There was a phone number and an address: 4040 Popohanni Lane; Kauai, Hawaii.

"Kauai. Some very expensive places on that island. Do you think this means Evan was selling these paintings to Henry Heckle?" I asked.

"Could be."

"If that's the case, then these other paintings were probably also forged and stolen, or are on Evan's 'to do' list."

"I'll contact the Kauai police and see what they can tell me about this Henry Heckle," Cavanaugh said. In the meantime, don't tell anyone else about this list or about the forgeries. I want to talk to a few people and see what they know before this becomes public knowledge."

I could think of a few people I wanted to talk to myself, including Henry Heckle.

I thought about talking to Cavanaugh about going to Kauai. I saw him telling me to stay put. I also thought about great works of art hanging in Kauai and forgeries circulating in our museums. I didn't think I wanted to wait around and just see what happened.

"I have some friends in Kauai," I said. "In fact, I've been visiting them for the past several years. I'll give them a call and see what they can find out about this Heckle fellow," I offered.

Cavanaugh gave me a warning look. "I won't mention the forgeries," I added, "I'll just get the scoop on this fellow."

"All right. Let me know what you find out. I'll do some checking with the local authorities there myself," Cavanaugh said. "In fact, if I hurry, I can probably still reach someone there today. They're four hours behind us. So, it's only two o'clock," Cavanaugh said. He gathered the photos and notebook, tucked them under his arm and left, saying, "I'll be in touch."

Chapter Fifteen

Mr. Postman, Look and See

I closed the door behind Cavanaugh and ran to my computer. As it churned through its opening sequences, I considered the searches I wanted to do. Henry Heckle, of course. And 4040 Popohanni Lane, in Kauai. I wished I'd made a copy of the list of paintings and names from Evan's notebook. Maybe I could find some connection between the people listed there. I made a mental note to myself to call Cavanaugh in a little bit.

As soon as the computer screen was up, I googled Henry Heckle. Wow! This fellow had five pages of listings. A lot of them related to a company called IN2NET. I clicked on one of the listings and was sped along the information highway to IN2NET's homepage. Henry Heckle's name appeared on nearly every page. He is IN2NET's founder and chairman. There was a brief description of what the company did, but its techno-talk left me in the dark. It was something about routers and information storage. Brave new world, here we come.

Then I searched 4040 Popohanni Lane, Kauai. Nothing for that address, but several real estate listings on Popohanni Lane came up. I clicked on one of them. Wow again! This was some neighborhood! The first listing price was $10 million. We're talking estate, not house, here. The ocean views were spectacular. The place had its own beach and ten acres filled with tropical gardens. Kauai is called the Garden Island because of its lush vegetation. And this was one garden I'd like to see in person. In fact, an idea was forming.

I clicked on my favorite travel site and checked the flight schedules to Kauai. American has a direct flight from O'Hare to Kauai leaving at 9 a.m. daily. With a three hour drive, an hour to check in, and an hour cushion, I'd have to leave here at 4 a.m. Ugh! But you know what, I just might do that. Tomorrow would be Wednesday. If I caught that 9 a.m. flight, I could be in Kauai by 1 p.m. Wednesday afternoon. The four hour time change really helped, at least on the trip there. That would leave me Wednesday evening and all day Thursday to check out Mr. Heckle and his art collection.

I made a few more clicks on the computer. Ever the optimist, I checked out Thursday's return flights. The last flight for O'Hare left Kauai at 10 p.m., getting me into O'Hare at 6 a.m. If I caught that Thursday evening flight back, I'd still be able to give my talk Friday night at the GAM opening. I might be giving it in my sleep after all that flying, but at least I'd be there! I made up my mind.

With a few more clicks on the keyboard, I'd booked my flights and even selected my seats. I hated to pay last minute prices for airline tickets but I had to take this trip. And what was the point of winning the lottery if I couldn't do the things I felt I really needed to do? Hey, I hadn't chartered a plane; this was public transportation we're talking here. Guess I just hate to waste money.

A few minutes later I checked my email, and there were my tickets. As I printed the e-ticket confirmations I marveled at how this little computer had changed our lives in the past few years. I sounded old, even to myself, thinking about it. But I guess that's how it happens. You live long enough to see the world evolve around you, and you either keep pace with the changes or you're left to rust in the field like the abandoned farm equipment you see around here. I, for one, planned to keep pace with the changes as long as I could! Bring on those e-tickets! I'll print them!

I threw a change of clothes, a few toiletries and my digital camera in a light carry-on bag and set my alarm for 3:30 a.m. I was about to get ready for an early bedtime when the door bell rang. Good heavens, I'd forgotten about Ken and Baxter! I ran to the bathroom mirror, put a brush through my hair, straightened my sweater, and flew down the stairs. I slowed myself as I got halfway across the kitchen, and walked to the front door with my heart pounding. "Jeez, would you relax," the little voice in my head said, as I turned the bolt and opened the front door.

Ken was standing there with Baxter at his side, a Gourmet Kitchen bag in one hand and several envelopes in the other. "Figured I'd save you the trip up to the road," he said, offering my mail to me.

"Thanks! Come on in," I said, taking the little bundle of letters as I opened the door wider. Truffs had heard the commotion, and was now standing behind my ankles. As Baxter came into the foyer behind Ken, Truffs gave one of her all time loudest protests, in the form of a hair-raising hiss, bared teeth and unsheathed claws.

"Truffs!" I said, quite taken aback, although it was clearly my fault for not tucking her away in a room. What was I thinking! Baxter backed up and gave a bark that shook the windows. "Great start," I thought. I scooped up Truffs, offering apologies as I dashed her from the room. "I'll be right back. Make yourself comfortable," I said, as Truffs squirmed and gave another giant hiss for good measure. I dashed upstairs, shut Truffs in my bedroom, and rejoined my company.

Ken and Baxter had settled themselves in the living room, Ken on the big yellow sofa and Baxter at his feet.

"Sorry about that," I said, taking a seat in my favorite chair.

Ken laughed and said, "Poor Truffs," then he recited: "Fare thee well, nymph. Ere he do leave this grove, Thou shalt fly him, and he shall seek thy love."

"That's Shakespeare, isn't it?"

"Yes. Oberon, in Midsummer's Night Dream. I must admit, Shakespeare's works are one of my true loves in life."

"Interesting, a Coast Guard Captain who loves Shakespeare! I do too, actually. Have you been to Stratford-on-Avon?" I asked.

"Both Stratfords, actually. I've been to the Stratford in London and our own continental version in Canada. How about you?"

"Just the Canadian version. Actually, I drive up there every August. The rose gardens are in full bloom, and I love walking along the river there."

"And the restaurants are phenomenal, aren't they?" he added.

"They certainly are. I have to diet for a week before I go and a week after I come back just to stay even!" I said, laughing, and finding myself studying the crinkles that formed around his eyes when he laughed. "When did you become a Shakespearian buff?" I asked.

"Goes back to college English days. I fell in love with the Bard's plays back then and have been talking about him ever since."

"Talking about him?" I said, not quite understanding what he meant.

"I taught English Lit at Clarke for years. Just retired, as a matter of fact, but still teach a few classes as an adjunct," he said.

"And when did the boating come in?" I asked.

"I've been in the reserves since I finished my Ph.D. I learned piloting there and have been doing it ever since. After I retired from full time teaching, I upped my commitment to the Coast Guard. It seemed to help fill the void after Melissa died."

"I'm sorry. Melissa was your wife?"

Ken turned from me and looked out the window then said, "Yes, she died of breast cancer, two years ago this September."

"How awful for you. How long were you married?"

"Eighteen years. We'd met in college. She was an English Professor, as well, at Loras College, in Dubuque."

"You must miss her very much."

"I do, but I don't usually talk about it. Don't know what's gotten into me here," he said, blushing.

"Not at all," I said. "We're just getting to know each other and it's an important part of who you are. Thank you for sharing with me," I said, meaning every word.

Ken gave Baxter's head a rub. "Well, I just wanted to say hello, since we were out this way."

"How did Baxter do at the vet's?" I asked, trying to get the conversation back on a lighter tone. I think we both needed the break.

"He did fine. Thanks." Ken cleared his throat. "So, why don't you tell me what Detective Cavanaugh had to say while we eat our salads?" he said, lifting the bag on the table in front of him.

"Yes, good idea. Let's sit at the table then," I said, rising and leading the way into the kitchen. As we ate, I filled him in: "Detective Cavanaugh found some photos of paintings and a list of names. There might be a connection with the paintings we found at the mine."

"What mine?" he asked looking confused.

"Oh, yes, I guess I thought you knew somehow, through the Coast Guard."

"They don't keep me informed on the progress of an investigation. I'm just running the search boat, not the investigation," he said and shrugged.

I shared the events of the past two days: Peter's GAM office, the memos, the paintings in the mineshaft, the crazy boyfriend, the whole thing. By the time I was finished, my throat was dry from all the talking. "How about something to drink?" I suggested.

"Sure. Tea would be great," he said.

Tea? I'd been thinking about a good strong scotch myself, but decided to join him in an herbal tea. As I went to the stove to put the water on to boil, I noticed my mail sitting on the counter where I'd put it when I'd dashed by to take Truffs upstairs. I picked up the little stack of envelopes and shuffled through them as I waited for the water to boil. The first two were credit card offers which I tore in half and tossed into the compactor without opening. The third was a hand addressed envelope without a return address. The stamp was cancelled in Chicago. I couldn't think who it would be from and assumed it had to do with Turning Points. I'd been getting letters from people wanting to apply for a grant ever since the article announcing the Foundation ran in the Chicago Tribune last year. I opened the letter, thinking I'd be sending it on to Polly's secretary with a note to send along a grant application, when I gasped. The signature was Peter's!

> *"Dear Karen,*
>
> *Yes, I am alive. I am sorry for all of the trouble and concern I have caused you. I am trusting you to keep this letter secret. I just want you to know I will be taking care of my dear wife and daughter. They will be joining me shortly. I would not have written except that I read about poor Lois in the paper as I waited for my plane to Italy. Please know that I had nothing to do with her death. I must leave Galena now, and forever. Dirk has uncovered a past secret, which would ruin me here. You see, in my school days, I was involved in a tragic accident. If you do some research you'll find out, but I would rather it remain forgotten. Thank you for everything you have done for me. I appreciated the opportunity to come back to my roots, even though I cannot stay. Let me disappear, if you can find it in your heart to do that.*
>
> *Love,*
>
> *Peter"*

Oh my God! What in the world was this all about? My mind whirled in circles. Thank heavens I hadn't read this before Cavanaugh arrived. At least it gave me time to figure out what I wanted to do. Could I honor Peter's request for secrecy and still find out what happened to Lois? Certainly the latter would take precedence, but could I do both?

"So what are you going to do about the fellow in Kauai?" Ken asked, walking over to the stove to join me. I composed myself and put Peter's letter in my pocket.

"Actually, I'm going to fly there tomorrow and see what I can find out in person. I don't think there's any way to find out what this fellow Heckle's involvement is from here."

"Well, if you need me to do anything for you while you're away, just let me know."

"Thanks. I will. In fact, there might just be," I said.

"Are you all right?" Ken asked looking at me strangely. "You look like you've seen a ghost."

"I have," I wanted to say, but didn't. He didn't know how close to the truth he was. "I'm just tired," I said.

"You know what, I think I'll take a rain check on that tea," Ken said. "If you're flying out tomorrow morning, I think you can use all the sleep you can get. Baxter and I'll head home. But I mean it, anything you need, you just call. Do you have my cell number?" he asked.

"I don't think I do."

He took out a card from his wallet, wrote his cell and home phone numbers on the back, and handed it to me. "Here," he said, "and I mean it, call me if you need anything"

He reached over and gave me a kiss on the cheek. I was shocked, pleased and confused at the same time. "Thanks," was all I managed to say, as I saw Ken and Baxter out the front door.

I'd wanted to tell Ken about Peter's letter, but I didn't want to break Peter's trust. How could Peter put me in a position like this! And what about Cavanaugh? Shouldn't I tell him? I figured I'd talk to Graziella first and see what she could tell me about this. I poured the water out of the tea kettle and watched it swirl down the kitchen drain. Man, was I tired.

I called Graziella and got her on the third ring. I told her about Peter's letter, and asked her what in the world was going on. I got the story between sobs. Peter and Graziella had planned Peter's disappearance. On Saturday afternoon, before our boat excursion, they'd left a small rowboat and dry clothes for Peter on the island in the River. When Peter jumped off the paddleboat on Sunday, he swam to the island, changed clothes, and rowed to shore. As part of their plan, Peter and Graziella had also purchased an old beater of a car and left it at the boat landing the day before. So after Peter rowed to shore, he got in the car and drove to O'Hare airport. His luggage, passport, and airline ticket for Italy were all waiting for him, locked in the trunk of the car. This time of year, no one was around to bother an old car sitting at the boat landing for a day. But then, Lois's unexpected tragic death had occurred. Graziella didn't know what to make of that. It certainly hadn't been part of their plan. That's why Graziella fainted when Lois's body was found. Between the stress of Peter's planned disappearance and Lois's death, it had all been too much for her. Graziella had received a letter from Peter today as well. Until then, she hadn't known for sure if he was all right. So she naturally was getting more and more upset with each passing day. Now, she was relieved. Part of Graziella and Peter's plan had been for Graziella to return to her family farm in Italy with Rosa and meet Peter there. Graziella told me she still planned to do that.

Well, at least I knew Peter was all right. Graziella begged me not to tell Cavanaugh. Apparently, she was afraid that Peter would be detained and probably tried and maybe even jailed. It turns out that in his college years, Peter encountered a crime in progress at a college party. Trying to stop the two fellows who were beating up another student, he grabbed a bronze figurine from the table next to him and hit one of the two fellows on the back of the head. The young man died in the emergency room. Peter was tried and convicted of involuntary manslaughter. He was sentenced to seven years probation, but fled the country. A warrant was issued for him, but he simply never returned to the United States—at least not until this past year. Dirk had found out about Peter's past and was using it to blackmail him.

Well, that explained a lot. Graziella repeatedly assured me that Peter had nothing to do with either Lois's death or the forgeries of the three paintings. I believed her, and based on that, I promised Graziella not to tell Cavanaugh about Peter's letter, at least not until after she and Rosa were back in Italy. If I could find out what had happened to Lois, and what Evan was planning to do with the three paintings, maybe we could let Peter's secret remain just that.

By the time we hung up, I was more exhausted than ever. And morning would come early. I marched upstairs went directly to bed, before anything else could happen. As I turned off my bedside light, Truffs wound her way into a comfy circle between my ankles. Well, comfy for her, anyway.

Chapter Sixteen

Aloha

The alarm went off as I was running along the beach towards a large house that kept getting frustratingly farther away. Groggily, I searched for the offending gadget, grabbed it and pressed the button down to stop the noise. I woke with that queasy feeling you get when you haven't had near enough sleep. Ick! Still, I slid my legs out from under Truffs, sat up on the side of the bed and switched on the light. "Sorry kiddo," I said, both to Truffs and myself.

I moved to the bathroom, splashed water on my face, and studied my reflection in the glare of the vanity lights. OK, I can do this. I jumped into the shower and was fully awake, dressed, and headed out the door in the next 15 minutes.

I drove down Blackjack to Sawmill. The dark country road twisted along, illuminated only by my headlights. Not even the farmhouses were lit yet. Another quarter hour and I was on two lane Highway 20 heading toward Chicago. Traffic increased to an occasional semi and my thoughts went to Peter. Not good. I made a voice note on my mini-recorder to call Bella. I knew she'd be keeping an eye on Graziella and Rosa. Not that there was much anyone could do, other than let Graziella know she had friends with her through all this. I wondered if Bella knew about Graziella and Peter's escape plan.

I decided to record what I knew so far, and see if saying it out loud gave me any new ideas about Lois. First, we had Lois fall or be pushed off the boat. Her ex-boyfriend was certainly odd enough, and obsessed enough, given that barrage of letters I'd found. And according to Dara he'd been in the parking lot by the *Mississippi Lady* on Sunday. Had he snuck on the boat to see her? Had he pushed her overboard in a fit of anger as the spurned lover?

And then there was her newly discovered birth family. Her brothers seemed genuinely happy to have a new member of the family. At least Fred was. Carter was definitely another odd one. But their sister sure had taken a dislike to Lois. Could there be sibling rivalry in a situation like this? Or was it the fear of having to share her mother's estate that had Rene so set against Lois? And how far would she have gone to protect what she saw as her birthright?

Then there was Lois's cryptic note to me at the Museum. In all likelihood, Lois had found the paintings in the mine. Was that what she and Evan were talking about on the boat? From the photos Detective Cavanaugh had found, it looked like Evan was the one who'd forged the paintings at the GAM. I figured he'd been the one to pass off my "Butterfly Bouquet" painting as a Dutch Master's work last year. I wondered what Evan had planned to do with the three paintings from the GAM. I hoped to get a clue from this fellow in Kauai.

I was at Rockford when the pink and gold dawn light began tinting the eastern sky. A few minutes later I swung onto Interstate 90 towards Chicago and was nearly blinded as the sun broke the horizon in a blaze of orange. A semi rolled up behind me going way above the speed limit. I could only hope he saw me in my little Boxster. He had to be fighting that same glare. The idiot! I breathed deeply and loosened the death grip I had on the steering wheel. Fear can give way to anger very easily. I did my yoga breath, pulling air into the bottom of my abdomen, filling it up and out to the top of my chest, releasing the air top down. I repeated this as the semi passed me.

Now I was humming along. I zipped through the first toll booth with my I-Pass. Three more tolls to go. They were spaced about every

20 minutes, so I'd be at O'Hare in one hour. Right on schedule. Traffic rolled along for about 40 minutes, and then came to a crawl, then a stop. I looked at my watch. I had two hours before the plane left and only ten miles to O'Hare. But that was no guarantee I'd make my plane. As I sat there, I prayed we'd start moving. It was six a.m. now, and I was surprised to hear the muffled ring of my cell phone coming from deep inside my travel purse.

I fumbled through my big leather bag, feeling my checkbook, wallet, airline ticket, Kleenex, lipstick, finally—the phone. "Hello," I said, hurrying to open the darn thing before it kicked into voice mail.

"Karen, it's Mark."

"Mark! Hi. You're up early, as usual."

"Just got back from my run. We didn't have much of a chance to talk yesterday, so I wanted to touch base before I headed for the office and got buried in meetings again."

"How nice of you," I said. Now, where to start! "Well, a lot's happened in the last 24 hours." I filled him in on the recent developments, and said: "So, I'm on my way to Kauai now, to find this Heckle fellow."

"What! Where are you?"

"I'm in the car, just outside O'Hare."

"Karen, be careful! Are you going with anyone? I mean, what do you think this fellow's going to do? Hand over all his stolen goods and say, I'm sorry?"

I paused. I didn't need this sarcasm. Deep breath. OK, so he's just worried about me and doesn't know how to deal with it. "I'll be all right, Mark. I'll call Janie and Linda when I get there. They'll put me in contact with the right people in the DA's office there, and then they'll get me through to the police. It'll be OK."

I was developing this plan as we spoke, and it wasn't a bad one! Janie and Linda were two law school friends of mine. They'd moved to Kauai shortly after graduation and had set up their law practice right there in paradise. I'm sure they'd be able to get me in touch with the local authorities.

"What about Cavanaugh?" Mark asked.

I paused. Should I tell him about Peter? "Tell you what, Mark. I'm going to retain you right now to represent me."

"To represent you in what?"

"Well, in this, this, case, or investigation, or what ever it becomes."

"What are you talking about, Karen?"

"Just say you'll represent me."

"OK, I'll represent you."

"All right, then what I'm going to tell you will be covered by attorney client privilege." And with that, I told Mark about Peter's letter.

"Oh, Karen," Mark said, in one long exhale. "You know you're withholding evidence, and maybe even helping a fugitive from the law?"

I paused. It didn't sound very good when he put it like that. "I'll tell you what. I promise to call Cavanaugh in 48 hours and tell him everything."

"And why not now?"

I paused again. The fact was, I wanted to give Graziella and Rosa time to catch their plane. But I didn't want to burden Mark with that bit of information. It would make his not calling Cavanaugh himself more difficult, so I just said, "I want to see what I can find out in Kauai first, before the police come storming in and this fellow makes off with whatever other stolen artwork he has."

"And how are you going to find out about whatever art work this fellow has?"

"I'll figure that out when I get there," I said. Translation: "You don't want to know." Actually, I had a plan. "Mark, I've got to pay attention to this traffic. I'll call you when I get there and know something."

"Be careful, Karen," Mark said again, and rang off.

The traffic started inching forward and I made my way off the interstate, into the O'Hare parking, at $36 a day, thank-you. Next I made my way through check-in, through two layers of security, and finally I was at the gate. I used the time before we boarded to call Tony and Louise, the couple who take care of Truffs and my place when I'm on the road, and often when I'm there. Then I called Graziella and let her know I'd promised to tell Cavanaugh on Friday about my letter from Peter. That at least gave her some time to catch her own plane, if that's what she was going to do. I called Bella and let her know she shouldn't worry if Graziella and Rosa decided to accelerate their travel plans, but didn't tell her anymore than that.

I left a message for Diane at the GAM asking her to cancel my appointment with Zeenie Zacks for this afternoon. I said I would be in touch later but not to worry, I would be there on Friday. It was way too early to call Linda and Janie. I'd have to do that from the plane.

Finally, we boarded—all 245 of us. The flight to Kauai was long and felt cramped, even in first class. But it was mercifully uneventful—something I greatly value in air travel. I used the time to catch up on the sleep I'd missed the past few days. Between naps, I worked on my approach with Heckle, and, ever the optimist, on my presentation for the GAM on Friday.

At 1:45 p.m. local time, we landed at Lihue. This is Kauai's only commercial airport and it's a complete contrast to O'Hare in everyway. First, there's the scale of things. Where O'Hare has planes coming in nonstop, you have four major flights a day arriving in Lihue. The whole Lihue terminal would fit in the restaurant space at O'Hare. Lihue is less than a quarter the size of even the Honolulu airport. Smaller isn't always better, but in this case, it definitely was. When you walk out of the terminal, you're greeted by the fragrantly flowering plumeria trees and singing birds. Plumeria are the white and yellow long lasting flowers used for leis. Their scent is heavenly, and being greeted with a lei forms a lasting impression of paradise.

I grabbed my suitcase off the turnstile and headed out the double doors. Janie was waiting for me in a white open top jeep, with mud splashed up the sides as if she'd just come from some off road adventure. She probably had. Kauai is known for its hiking and off road trails leading to the most glorious waterfalls in the world.

"Hey, girlfriend!" she said, waving and getting out of the car. We hugged "hello," laughing and smiling at our unexpected reunion. Actually, we'd just seen each other a few months ago, when I'd escaped the Jo Daviess February Freeze with a month's visit to the Garden Island. But we hadn't expected to see each other again until maybe next February, so there was a bit of added joy in the surprise of my return visit. That is until I had to explain why I was there. I recounted the whole story, *sans* Peter's letter, as we headed out of the airport.

"OK, so where do we go from here?" Janie asked.

"I think we need to talk to the local police," I said. "At least let them know what we're up to here, and see what they know about Henry Heckle."

"I know someone we can talk to," Janie said, nodding, and taking the right turn onto Kuhio Highway, a/k/a Highway 51. Hawaiian names can be confusing to us mainlanders. There are only 12 letters in the Hawaiian alphabet: five vowels (a, e, i, o and u) and seven consonants (h, k, l, m, n, p and w). And every consonant is followed by a vowel. It definitely takes some getting used to.

This road runs north and south along the east coast of the island and we were taking it north.

"It's three o'clock now," Janie said. "The surfers will just be coming in off Anini's Secret Beach. We'll catch Onono there, or at the Makai Ono Burger joint they all go to after surfing. Onono is the island Google. He knows all, or at least what's up on the North Shore,"

Janie laughed. "My guess is, he'll know what this Heckle fellow's about."

"And what about the police?"

"We'll talk to them after we talk to Onono. I think we'll know more what we're dealing with then," she said. On the way, Janie filled me in on her past two months, on her and Linda's practice, and on the story of how they'd met Onono. They were representing a shopping center developer, and Onono represented the group of native islanders opposed to the development. They'd worked out a deal that established a land sanctuary just west of Hanalei and east of Na Pali. It made sense to keep larger tracks of land undeveloped as opposed to a lot along a shore already lined with condominiums. So both sides were happy with the results. Onono and Janie had become friends, and he'd introduced her to some of the ancient Hawaiian customs honoring the ocean and the land.

We drove by Coconut Grove Shopping Center. The center takes its name from the large stand of 50 foot tall coconut palm trees planted some 60 years ago by the resort developer. I caught glimpses of waves and beach to my right as we headed up the coast. The ocean breeze felt great after the stuffy airplane air.

Sugar cane grew freely along the roadside. The sugar cane is a remnant of the massive sugar plantations that operated here until the 1970's. About mid-island, just at Wailua, I caught a glimpse of the double Wailua Falls. This is one of the most spectacular of the hundreds of waterfalls on Kauai. The Wailua River runs along an old dense lava flow then suddenly plunges 200 feet into pools of water below. The softer rock below is continually worn away by the constant flow of water. Eventually, the lip of the old lava flow is completely undercut and it crashes down. So the waterfall is continually creeping back inland, just like Niagara Falls.

I was still musing on these forces of nature when, a few minutes later, just past the town of Kapaa, the Nounou Ridge mountain peaks rose to my left.

"That mountain is called The Sleeping Giant," Janie said. "With a little imagination you can envision the mountain as a man lying on his back. Have you ever heard how the mountain got its name?" Janie asked.

"No."

"Well, according to Hawaiian folklore, when Kauai was in danger of being invaded by Oahu, the Menehunes sought the help of Puni, a very big and clumsy giant. They found him asleep on this ridge. They threw boulders on his stomach to wake him up, but he kept sleeping. Some of the rocks bounced off his stomach and hit several of the attacking canoes which sent the invaders fleeing. Unfortunately Puni swallowed a few of the rocks and died in his sleep. So there he still lies today."

"Great story," I said. "I love to hear the local legends. You know, on my last trip I heard that Sotheby's was offering five acre home sites along the Kapaa coast here, starting at $1.7 million."

"That's right. And they're selling out fast," Janie said. "It looks like Puni is going to have lots of company."

"Too bad for paradise," I said.

The vegetation changed as we headed north. The southern tip of the island is hot and dry. It's actually a desert. The northern coast is just the opposite. It's more like a tropical garden. Lush foliage, giant flowering trees, and cascading waterfalls line the highway. Just before Princeville, the major resort on the North Shore, we took a right on the first Kalihiwai Road. There are actually two Kalihiwai Roads. The bridge that once connected them was destroyed by a tsunami in 1957 and never replaced. That's probably one of the reasons this beach has remained a secret, well, secret from the tourists anyway. Locals have long used this as one of the best surf spots on the island. This and Tunnels Beach, by the Na Pali Coast, were the top surfers beaches.

Kalihiwai Road was seal coated at this point and twisted and turned past some gorgeous homes. A half mile later, the road narrowed and the seal coating ended. Now we were on a dirt road, rutted from the combination of tropical rain and cars. The homes we passed were smaller and closer together. A stray dog took exception to us and ran alongside the car barking. A homemade sign tacked to a tree urged us to "slow down." Janie braked as the proverbial chicken made its way across the road in front of us. Kauai's beaches and roadsides were filled with these colorful wild chickens, descendants of some long ago chicken coop escapees. The houses to our left had a rundown look to them. "For Rent" signs had been planted along the road in front of most of them, with plexiglass mailboxes offering flyers to prospective vacationers. The quarter mile long sand beach opened to our right.

Janie pulled over onto the mix of sand and dirt under a stand of ironwood trees that lined the edge of the beach. This was the surfers' parking lot. Rusted trucks with surfboard carriers strapped to their tops were parked at odd angles, wherever the trees permitted.

"This is it," Janie said. "Let's go!"

I gave my suitcase a glance, stashed in the back seat of the open jeep. Oh well. I spotted a towel on the floor, grabbed it, threw it over my belongings and scurried to catch up with Janie.

A large black lab ran circles around us as we walked the 50 yards to the shore. "Max, good boy," Janie said, grabbing a piece of driftwood and tossing it for this canine beach boy.

"Max is Onono's dog," Janie said. "So Onono is probably out there," she said, pointing to a dozen forms bobbing on the water about a quarter mile off shore. We watched the surfers lying on their stomachs on their boards, paddling with their arms, pulling themselves out beyond the breaking surf. They floated out there until the right wave came, then stood, and rode the crest of the wave back into shore. As we were standing there, a 50 something year old fellow with a stud earring, golden Hawaiian skin, and sparkling black hair and eyes rode his board onto the shore ten yards from us.

"Onono!" Janie exclaimed.

"Aloha, Janie!" Onono gave Janie the "hook 'em horns" gesture that meant hello in Hawaii, then grabbed his surf board and jogged over to us. He gave Janie a one armed wet embrace.

"This is my friend, Karen," Janie said, looking from Onono to me.

"Glad to meet you," I said, extending my hand.

Onono shifted his surf board from his right hand to his left hand and engulfed my extended hand in his. "Any friend of Janie's is a friend of mine," he said, radiating warmth.

"Thank you," was all I said, but I knew he'd help us if he could.

"Can we buy you a burger at Makai's?" Janie asked.

"Sure. Give me five to load up my board, and we'll meet you there," Onono said, petting Max.

"Great. We'll see you there, then," Janie said, and we headed back across the golden sand to our jeep.

We wound our way back up Kalihiwai and took a right towards Kilauea, home of the Kilauea Light House. The light house was built in 1913 to guide ships traveling between the West Coast of the United State and Asia. It sits on a 200 foot tall cliff at the edge of a promontory that is now a National Wildlife Refuge. The lighthouse boasts the largest clamshell-shaped lens in the world. But what I remember most from my tour of the lighthouse this past February are the wonderful birds that make this peninsula their home. There are albatross, frigate birds, shearwaters and actual red-footed boobies.

We crossed a long bridge and a dramatic two tiered waterfall came into view. I braced myself up in my seat to take in the sight as long as I could. When I turned back to look at the road Janie was slowing to take our turnoff.

Chapter Seventeen

The Collector

Makai Ono Burger turned out to be a sort of run down barn converted to a local burger joint. There was a sign large enough for tourists to see but the dilapidated look of the facility surely scared off all but the most adventuresome. There were tables outside, but Janie ignored them. We walked through the unpainted wooden door, through the packed bar/dining room and out the back into a tree shaded garden with just three tables. "*Makai*," it turns out, is the Hawaiian word for "towards the ocean." And this tucked away little spot had a gorgeous *makai* view. "*Ono*" is the Hawaiian word for "good." And Janie assured me the burgers here lived up to their name.

We ordered three cold beers and three burgers. The beers arrived just as Onono joined us.

"Hey Janie, thank you," he said, sliding onto the picnic table bench alongside her. "So what can I do for you two *wahini* today?" he asked with a smile.

"I need some information, Janie said. "And I'm sure you know everyone on this island and their mothers and brothers," she added with a laugh.

"Might be," he said, joining in her laughter. He obviously liked his unofficial Google role.

"Have you ever heard of a fellow named Heckle, Henry Heckle?" she asked.

"He lives on Popohanni Drive," I added, pulling the slip of paper with his address from my purse and sliding it across the table to Onono.

"Sure I know him, know of him, anyway," Onono said. "What do you want to know?"

"What does this fellow do? How does he make his money?" Janie asked.

"That's a very good question. He moved here about seven years ago. From California, is what I hear. Came with money; done nothing here to make money; and has a lot of it from what I see."

"So you think he's making his money illegally? Drugs or something?"

"This would be a crazy place to run drugs. Too small a community to do much here, but I don't think he's running a Fortune 500 business either."

"So, how do we find out what he's into?" Janie asked.

"We don't. I do," he said. "And I'll give you a call. I still have your cell number memorized," he said, his smile a nod to their past exchanges.

"OK," Janie said as the waitress brought out our burger baskets. We left it at that and dove into our Makai Ono burgers.

When we pulled out of the lot, I asked Janie to take me by Heckle's place. "It's up here in the Princeville area, isn't it?" I asked.

"It is. Popohanni Drive is right off the main entrance to the Princeville Resort, by the Queen's Bath."

"What's the Queen's Bath?" I asked.

"Nature's swimming pool," Janie said. "You've never been down there?"

"No."

"Well, it's named for Queen Emma, the most famous of the Hawaiian Queens. She and King Kamehameha IV ruled all of the islands in the mid 1800's, if I remember my Hawaiian history correctly. Princeville was actually named by a Scotsman, Robert Chrichton Wyllie, in 1860, after Queen Emma's son, Prince Albert. Wyllie was Hawaii's ambassador to the world for 20 years." Janie paused then said, "Once I get started on Hawaiian history it's hard to stop. Anyway, I was telling you about the Queen's Bath. It's really something to see. You climb down a steep cliff to an old lava flow. The ocean's waves crash against the coast and fill a 600 foot natural basin in a lava peninsula. The waters are supposed to have restorative powers."

"Just sitting next to the ocean has restorative powers," I said, longing to do just that. But time was way too short this visit and we had a lot of work ahead of us.

We took a right turn into the gated entrance to the Princeville Resort. A 50 foot statue of Poseidon stood atop four giant scalloped seashells. Water sprayed in wide arcs from the edge of the pool surrounding the statue and flowed into the shells. I loved this fountain, especially at night when the lights made it even more dramatic. We passed by the unmanned gate house, the guards only coming out at night due to the amount of traffic into the resort community. This was the home of the famed Princeville Hotel, five stories of marble clinging to the side of a cliff overlooking one of the most spectacular ocean bays in the world. I'd spent a wonderful two weeks there but that too is a story for another time.

"You know, there was once a Russian fort here on the same bluff the Princeville Hotel is on today. It was called Fort Alexander and was built in 1816. But the Hawaiians drove them off the island after just a few months. You can still see the grassy mound that was the fort's perimeter." Janie was a fount of knowledge and that always made it interesting to be with her.

To our right and left were the four Princeville golf courses: the famed Prince Course, (no relation), rated number one in the Islands; and the Makai Lakes, Ocean and Woods Courses The later three, unlike the Prince, were actually playable by the recreational golfer, like me.

Condominiums were creeping into the green spaces of this resort at an alarming rate. Every year the ratio slid in favor of bricks and mortar. This was great for the price of real estate and not so great for those of us searching for a beautiful natural setting, including the albatross. One of these beautiful big white, black and grey birds swooped into a mowed green space along the side of the road. My heart went out to this gorgeous creature as I saw it land near a ten foot circle of unmowed grass in the center of the city block sized lawn. Its mate raised its head and I could just see a downy, smaller version of the birds poke its head up alongside its waiting mother. What must the poor birds have thought as the lawn mower made circles around their nest. And how brave to have stood their ground. Albatross have been returning to the island to nest for centuries. My guess was you could count on your right hand the number of years this green space would be left for them to return to.

We took the first right and followed the winding paved road past low rise condominium developments surrounded by rows and rows of flowering red hibiscus bushes. Great stands of birds of paradise plants bore brilliant orange sepals and blue, arrowhead-shaped flowers rising out of a green and red bract that looks like a bird's head. The bird of paradise is actually a South African plant. But it is so commonly used in Hawaii that visitors think it's a Hawaiian native species.

Soon the condominiums gave way to single family homes. We were working our way out to the edge of a promontory and as we approached the coastline, I was surprised to see there were no homes along the shore. A large white fence ran along the perimeter of what appeared to be a private estate. Thirty foot tall Kou trees covered in orange blossoms marked the entrance. Two carved marble statues of ancient Hawaiian warriors stood on either side of a closed gate barring the driveway. 4040 Popohanni Lane was chiseled on a pillar to the right of the gate.

"So what do you think?" I asked, looking at Janie. "Now or later?"

Janie took a deep breath and looked back at me, "Hey, no time like the present."

I noticed a camera positioned at the top of one of the towering statues. I hoped no one was watching us sitting there discussing out strategy.

"Well, do we call? Do we both go in or just me?" I tossed out questions.

"Let's call, then you go in and I'll wait for you. Better to have one of us on the outside I think—just in case."

"Good idea."

I pulled out my cell phone and called information for the number. Private listing. Darn! But I guess I should have figured that. If you have ten acres on this coast you probably don't want to be bothered by sales people, or ladies from the Midwest looking for stolen art.

"Well, tell you what. I'll drop you at the Princeville Hotel, and come back here myself. If I'm not back in an hour, come find me. And bring help," I said.

"And how would I do that if you have my car?" she countered.

"Well, what do you suggest?"

"I'll drop you off at the front door, chauffer style, and come back to get you when you call. I'll just wait over at the hotel."

"All right," I said. It wasn't the smoothest plan I'd ever heard but it worked with what we had available to us just then, which was the two of us and one car.

We pulled into the driveway and stopped at the pillar with the chiseled address. There was a speaker embedded in the pillar at car window height. How convenient—except that I wanted to be the one talking, not Janie. We climbed over each other and switched seats, awkward but not impossible since the jeep was *sans* roof. Man, I hoped no one was watching us.

I pressed the brass button and stared at the speaker waiting for a voice. There was a crackle, then, a disembodied but lyrical woman's voice said: "Aloha. Can I help you?"

"Aloha," I responded, giving back the traditional Hawaiian greeting. "I'm Karen Prince, and I'm looking for Mr. Henry Heckle."

"Yes, Mr. Heckle is expecting you?"

"Well, no, actually, but I think he'd like to talk to me." It never hurts to be positive.

"May I tell him what you would like to see him about?"

"Yes, of course. We share a love of fine art. I would like to talk to him about a very special painting." I find it's easier to stay as close to the truth as possible at all times.

"One moment please, Ms. Prince."

"Are you sure you don't want me to come with you?" Janie asked, as we waited for the woman to talk to Heckle and, I hoped, buzz us in.

"I'd rather have someone on the outside know I was in there, to tell you the truth." I could see Janie didn't want to miss out on the excitement, and living here, she was probably dying to get a look inside this mansion.

"Tell you what, I'll just call Linda right now, and let her know where we are and what we're doing, and then we'll be covered."

Well that would probably work, if Linda wasn't with a client or in court. "Oh, all right, give her a call," I said. "If you can reach her, then come in with me."

Janie had already pressed the speed dial number for their office before I'd finished talking.

Apparently she'd dialed Linda's direct number because it didn't sound like she was talking to a secretary. "Hey. I picked up Karen and we're about to meet a fellow called Henry Heckle. Got that? Here, write down this address. This is where we'll be: 4040 Popohanni Lane. Right by Queen's Bath in Princeville. We should be here about a half hour, then I'll call you and we can get together for dinner. And Linda, if I don't call you in half an hour, you're going to have to come looking for us. I'm serious."

There was a pause on Janie's side of the conversation. Janie turned to me and said: "Linda says 'hello and she'll back us up'."

"Tell her I say hello, back." Janie had nerves of steel. I guess going into this place was more exciting than scary to her. I had to say the equation tipped a bit the other way for me.

There was a bit of static from the speaker box, and then the same lyrical voice said, "Mr. Heckle will see you. *Mahalo*." The gates swung open ahead of us.

As we drove down the drive in our mud-spattered jeep, a stone mansion came into view. It was primarily sheets of glass and stone formed into a low angular structure. It reminded me of Wright's *Falling Water*, without the stream. The place was a work of art. The gardens lining the drive were a manicured masterpiece and formed a backdrop to four massive stone carvings. They had the feel of ancient Hawaiian carvings and, given their surroundings, they were probably just that.

We pulled through a circle drive to the parking area just to the right of the house. The same lyrical voice greeted us as we walked up to the front door.

A young woman, who appeared to be about 18, Hawaiian, and drop dead gorgeous, beckoned us into the house. "Have a seat in the library, please. Mr. Heckle will be with you soon," she said, gesturing to the room to our left.

This was not your typical dark wood paneled library. Floor to ceiling white wood shelves lined the east wall. The other three were covered in gold fabric, and bore what appeared to be three large Monet water scenes. I gasped. I'd seen many of Monet's original water scenes in Paris, at the Musee d'Orsay and L'Orangerie. And of course, I'd studied the haystack series and the Notre Dame series at the Art Institute of Chicago, thanks to the acquisitive Mrs. Bertha Honore Palmer. And, I have to say, these paintings had all of the subtle color variations and shimmering light of those glorious works. I noticed the temperature and humidity gauges on the wall. Heckle was serious about creating the proper environment to preserve his collection. My guess was they were the real thing. So we were looking at about $30 million worth of art here. Just a ballpark figure, of course.

Janie and I were lost in reverie, standing side by side looking at the largest of the three paintings, when a deep voice behind us said: "Admiring my collection, I see."

We turned in unison to see a small man, not more than five feet tall, with oval rimless glasses and short cropped hair.

"One of you is Ms. Prince, I presume?" he asked.

"I am," I said, stepping forward to shake his hand. He stared at me, and left my hand hanging in mid-air, unmet. I dropped it and took a step back.

"This is my friend and lawyer, Ms. Jane Mac Masters."

"Does this visit require your lawyer, Ms. Prince?"

"I have a business proposition I'd like to discuss with you."

"Perhaps I should have my own counsel with me then?" he said with a chuckle that implied he didn't feel he needed advice to deal with me.

"That is, of course, up to you. Perhaps you could hear my proposal yourself and then decide," I said.

Heckle nodded and walked to the glass table in the middle of the room. "Won't you have a seat?" he said, sitting at the head of the table himself.

Janie and I sat side by side in the chairs closest to him. I hated these power games, and I wasn't going to be intimidated by this fellow or his trappings.

Heckle stared at me, waiting for me to say something, which I did.

"Mr. Heckle, I have recently learned that we have several things in common: a love of art and the wherewithal to indulge our passion," I said.

"Indeed. How did you come to hear that?" he asked. "You are from? Where? Not here, certainly."

"No, I'm from the Midwest," I said. "A small town called Galena." I could visibly see him lose interest. He shifted his body weight and looked at the paintings behind us.

"I have recently won the lottery," I had his attention again, "and am looking at acquiring several paintings for my own collection. I was visiting my friend, here, and she told me you would be the best person on the Island to talk to about—acquisitions."

His eyes narrowed as he looked from me to Janie and back to me again. "Perhaps," he said. "What did you have in mind?"

"I'm particularly interested in Dutch master floral paintings," I said. "But they are rare, and hard to come by."

"Indeed they are," he said.

"And I also have a particular interest in Martin Johnson Heade's works, particularly his landscapes and orchids. You are familiar with his work, I presume?"

Heckle laughed, a somewhat hysterical laugh that sent a chill down my spine. Janie and I looked at each other.

Heckle pushed his chair back, "Come!" he said. Then he stood and marched from the room without looking back. Janie and I looked at each other, shrugged, and followed Heckle down the hall.

We passed a dinning room, an office, and entered a room I can only describe as a museum quality gallery. Paintings hung European style, one above another, covering nearly all available wall space. I gasped!

"What a collection!" I said. I was truly in awe.

"Thank you," Henry said, walking to one of the four wingback chairs forming a seating group in the center of the room. "Take your time," he said to us as we began walking slowly around the room. There were several floral paintings which appeared to be from my favorite Dutch period, mid 1600's to 1700.

"Is this a Bossecart?" I asked, stopping in front of a beautiful depiction of flowers in a window niche with blue sky and rolling hills behind it.

"Yes, it is," Heckle said. "You have a very good eye."

"As I said, art is my passion, especially floral art. This work is truly a gift from above. A crystallization of grace and beauty for all time," I said and I meant it.

Henry had opened a wireless laptop which was sitting on the glass table in front of him. He clicked away, seemingly oblivious to us.

"I see you did indeed win the Lottery," Heckle said.

I turned, startled. "You googled me?"

"I did. Simple matter of knowing whom you are dealing with. A basic principal of business, wouldn't you say?"

"Yes. And you, Ms. Mac Masters, office in Lihue. That's the new office building on Main Street isn't it?

Seems he was doing his background check right there in front of us. Well, I couldn't blame him. It was actually a smart move on his part.

"What did we do before the internet?" Janie remarked.

"We relied on personal referrals. We didn't drop in without a reference."

So the man was blunt, if nothing else. I was glad I'd chosen to use my own name. I figured he'd check somehow. I just didn't know it would be that quickly.

"What are you interested in acquiring, Ms. Prince? Perhaps I can help put you in touch with the right people."

If I'd really wanted to acquire a painting, I'd be going to an auction or to a gallery specializing in the type of art I wanted to acquire. But I suppose this sort of personal brokerage occurred as well. "I'd be particularly interested in acquiring a Heade. He painted the most extraordinary floral still lifes and landscapes as well."

"I am quite familiar with Heade's work," Heckle said, in an overly emphatic tone.

Oops. I think I just insulted our host. "Of course, of course. It's just that I don't think one's come on the market since the National Gallery had its solo show of his work in 2000."

"Not many change hands, it's true. But, I may be able to help you, if you are willing to pay what such a master work is worth."

"I would suggest we talk price when we are talking about a specific work," I said. "A specific painting would mean a great deal more to me than any other."

"Which is that, if I may ask?" Heckle said.

Janie had taken a seat across from Heckle, and I moved to stand closer to him.

"The *Orchids and Hummingbirds*," I said.

Heckle's jaw clenched and his eyes narrowed. He reached out and grabbed my wrist with his left hand and yanked me into the chair next to him. "Where did you say you were from, Ms. Prince? Galena, did you say?"

"That's right," I gasped, the air knocked out of me. Heckle still had a death grip on my right wrist. My hand was turning red from the pressure. Apparently I'd tripped some sort of alarm in Heckle's personal protection system and it looked like he wasn't buying my story. Heckle reached into his jacket pocket with his right hand and pulled out a small black gun. He aimed it at my head and let go of my wrist.

My eyes were glued to him. Was he nuts? What was he going to do? Shoot me right there in his sitting room?

A voice I recognized boomed behind me. "This little charade is over, Karen!"

I turned. Dirk was standing in the doorway.

"Dirk! How did you—"

"How did I get here?" Dirk said, cutting me off. "Same as you. I was right there on the plane. Followed you, in fact. You didn't notice the bearded rabbi way back there in coach class, I suppose?

No, I hadn't.

"Evan called me the minute he found the paintings were gone from the mine. Silly of you to take them, my dear. Tipped your hand, you know."

I looked over at Janie. She had her hand in her purse on her lap. But she was staring at Dirk and I couldn't catch her eye.

"Sorry, Janie" I thought. Just then she raised her purse in the air with her hand still in it. There was an incredibly loud sound, then Dirk screamed and grabbed his shoulder. I used the chaos as cover. I swung my arm up and knocked the gun from Heckle's hand. It flew across the room, skidding across the wooden floor and hitting the wall with a thump.

Janie and I dashed to the door back to the hallway. Heckle was on his feet in a flash and right behind us. We tore out of the house, jumped into the jeep, and sped out the drive.

"Where the heck did you get that gun?" I gasped.

"You could say, thank you," Janie said without taking her eyes off the road. She was doing at least 50 miles an hour down the driveway. The jeep's tires screeched and gravity threw me against the passenger door as Janie yanked the wheel and got us back onto Popohanni Lane. I laughed in sheer relief.

"OK. Thank you," I said. Suddenly we were rammed from the rear! I was thrown into the dash board and hit my head on the windshield. I slumped to the floor then peeked back over the front seat. Heckle was following us! At least there was a black Mercedes right on our tail.

I looked over at Janie. She was scrunched down as low as she could behind the wheel. She looked like a kid stealing a car. A shot rang out. "Keep down!" we both yelled and looked at each other. Nervous laughter was a transparent cover for our sheer terror.

We were back in the condo development area leading to the main road in the Princeville Resort. A jogger in paradise made a 90 degree turn and took off running away from us as fast as he could as another shot rang out.

"Someone's going to get hurt if Heckle doesn't cut it out!" I yelled to Janie over the screech of our tires. She turned right onto Princeville Drive. Apparently we weren't leaving the complex! We passed the eighth hole of the Lakes Course. A fellow was on the tee box preparing to hit. I couldn't imagine that the whole world wasn't focused on us. But somehow we were only a tiny spot of activity among millions of interlocking universes. And theirs were apparently much more peaceful than ours.

We swerved to pass one of the white convertibles that 90 percent of the tourists rent in Kauai. A line of slow moving white convertibles lay ahead of us. Couples walking along the hibiscus lined path leading to the resort stopped and pointed. The black Mercedes jumped the curb, passed the white convertible we'd just passed, and rammed into our right rear fender. The jeep leaped into the oncoming traffic lane. Janie hit the accelerator. We sped across the road, just missing another jeep, bounced up the curb and onto the walking path on the other side of the road. Horns blared and walkers scattered, grabbing trees for protection. The black Mercedes was right behind us.

"Hang on," Janie yelled, as we wove between the eucalyptus tree trunks forming the barrier between the walking path and the golf course.

"I am!" I yelled back. The Mercedes followed us through the eucalyptus trees. The wrenching sound of twisting metal mixed with pedestrians' screams. The Mercedes' passenger side had taken a hit but Heckle was still behind us.

Janie shifted into four wheel drive and headed for the cart path. Stunned golfers stopped and pointed. "Where are you going?" I shouted to Janie from my position on the floorboards.

"To the Ocean's third hole" she yelled back.

"Golfing?" I asked .

"You'll see," she said as we sped down the cart path along the second fairway to the next hole. Just past the third tee the cart path narrowed and took a sharp turn down a steep incline. We bounced over the speed bumps as the Mercedes rounded the corner behind us and started down. Jungle lined both sides of the path. The Mercedes made the first turn but skidded on the second, veered into the jungle and careened downhill. The trees and vines took the worst of it. The Mercedes headed for the bottom of the ravine. We kept going, crossed over a stream and followed the twisting cart path back up the ravine.

"We can cut over here to the hotel," Janie said, cutting the wheel so sharply we spun a donut. The force sent Janie's purse flying off the seat onto the floor next to me.

"Your cell phone in here?" I yelled as Janie slowed to straighten out the jeep and then accelerated again heading toward the coastline.

"You want to chat now?" she asked, her voice bobbing as we hit the speed bumps on the cart path signaling the turn around at the cliff's edge.

"I'll call Linda and have her tell the hotel security we're heading there. She can get the Island police to pick up our two friends."

"Right," she yelled, now going cross country along the jagged coastline toward the hotel in the distance.

Chapter Eighteen

To Friends

Linda, Janie and I sat on the terrace looking out at Hanalei Bay. We'd just given our sworn statements to Detective Molokono and promised to be available for any other questions he might have. Linda and Janie's years of law practice in the community went a long way toward easing his concerns about me as a flight risk. It also lent credibility to my story of art thefts and shoot-outs.

"The police found Heckle unconscious in his car," Linda said. "And they picked up Dirk at the emergency room. The bullet had lodged in his shoulder, so he didn't have much of a choice but to get it tended to. He gave them some story about an accidental shooting."

"It was some story all right," I said, raising my glass to Janie. "To friends!" I said.

"To friends," they repeated. We each took a sip of champagne.

Talk about friends, I called Bella after I talked to Detective Molokono, and filled her in on what had happened here. She told me that Cavanaugh had arrested Evan for stealing the three paintings from the GAM. Once he was arrested, Evan broke down and told Cavanaugh the whole story. Evan admitted to the forgeries but not to killing Lois. Lois had confronted Evan on the boat on Sunday. That was the scene I'd watched unfold. Unfortunately, Evan told his father that Lois had caught on about the forgeries. Dirk warned Lois to keep quiet, but when he saw her talking to me, Dirk decided to act, then and there. Evan saw Dirk hit Lois on the head with one of the boat's fire extinguishers and then throw Lois over the side of the boat. Dirk had returned the fire extinguisher to its glass case on the side of the boat after he'd used it. He probably wanted Lois's death to look like an accident and a missing fire extinguisher would have raised a red flag. Detective Cavanaugh would undoubtedly find traces of blood and hair on the fire extinguisher now that he knew where to look.

Evan hadn't intended to harm anyone, at least not physically. Forgery and fraud he rationalized as vague crimes against unknown individuals or companies. Evan also told Cavanaugh that Dirk had been embezzling money from several of his clients' trust accounts. Dirk had desperately needed money to repay the trust accounts before the audit of his law firm's books. I remembered Diane telling me that Dirk had missed his meeting with his auditors on Monday. Apparently he'd been trying to put off the audit until he'd replenished the trust accounts. The story Bella heard was that Dirk thought he'd solved his problems when his client, Zeenie Zacks, came to him. Zeenie Zacks wanted more money than the three percent interest the Willow Trust could legally pay her. She had come to Dirk, as her attorney, to see if she could force the Willow Trust to distribute its assets to her. Dirk confirmed that the terms of the trust agreement did not authorize the sale of trust's assets for another ten years, just as John Harris, the trust officer, had told her. But ten years was much longer than Zeenie wanted to wait. So Dirk found a loophole—if the trust's assets were lost or stolen, the insurance proceeds would be distributed to her as sole beneficiary of the trust. And Dirk offered to make that happen. He arranged to sell the three original paintings to Heckle, with Dirk and Zeenie splitting the sale proceeds. After the *Flowers in Art Exhibit* had left the GAM, Dirk would arrange for an appraisal of the trust's three paintings on Zeenie's behalf. When they were discovered to be forgeries, Dirk and Zeenie would split the insurance proceeds as well. Quite a plan—except that it didn't work. Detective Cavanaugh had arrested Zeenie Zacks. Dirk was in custody and would be flown back to Galena and charged with Lois's murder.

Bella also told me that Graziella and Rosa had left for Italy yesterday. Apparently Cavanaugh was none too happy about their leaving with Peter still missing, but there wasn't any way he could make them stay.

"So they'll be with family soon," Janie said. I debated telling Linda and Janie about Peter's letter, but just said, "Yes, they will," and left it at that.

I didn't think Dirk could do much with his information about Peter now that Peter was out of the country. It wasn't like Peter was a threat to society, so I didn't see the international police dragging him back to Galena. I was sorry I hadn't been able to say goodbye. But who knows, maybe someday I'd be traveling to Italy and would stop by and see them and their family farm. You never know what adventures lay ahead.

"To the future," I said.

"To the future," Linda and Janie echoed, our toast punctuated by the clink of our champagne glasses.

Epilogue

Summertime, and the Living is Easy

I'd made it back from Kauai in time for my presentation at the GAM's opening reception that Friday night in May. After that, the Board asked me to serve as Director of the Museum until they found a replacement for Peter. The Museum's attendance has surpassed all of our expectations. The murder-forgery story was covered not only in the Midwest but throughout the entire country. I understand we made the evening network news, as well as the headlines on Yahoo.

Mark couldn't make it out for the opening, but Ken did. He's also volunteered to take over the GAM Newsletter and be our media representative, filling in until Lois's replacement is hired. Bella's business has taken off. We've hired her to do lunches at the GAM while the *Flowers in Art Exhibit* is here. Between that and private catering events, she's successfully launched her new career.

As a result of the press coverage, Bella's been asked to cater the Asheville Horseshow at the Biltmore Estate. Well, as a result of the press coverage and the fact that our mutual friend, Tissy, organizes the show. The Biltmore mansion has a fully equipped kitchen and staff. So all Bella will have to do is fly down there and prepare her wonderful recipes.

Bella and Tissy have both invited me to come to North Carolina to see the show. It's supposed to be quite an event. And, you know, I could use a nice quiet diversion. So, I just might do that.

Bella's Best Recipes

Spring Asparagus and Morel Mushrooms

1/2 pound morel mushrooms
2 tablespoons olive oil
1 pound asparagus (24 stalks)
1 loaf Italian bread
1/8 cup olive oil
Salt and pepper
1/4 cup grated Parmesan cheese

Trim the morels, giving each stem a clean cut. Slice morels in half lengthwise and soak them in a large bowl of water. Change the water until all dirt is removed. Drain morels on a clean towel. Sauté the morels in 2 tablespoons olive oil until they are deep brown and all moisture is evaporated from the pan. The morels will be a caramel brown color.

Rinse the asparagus. Remove bottoms of spears leaving 4 inch long top pieces. Steam the asparagus over boiling water just until tender. Remove the asparagus immediately.

Preheat broiler. Cut 12 slices of bread, ½ inch thick. Broil bread on a baking sheet for several minutes until lightly browned. Remove from oven, turn toasted side down. Drizzle top of each slice with olive oil and sprinkle with salt and pepper. Return to broiler another minute until this side is browned. Remove from oven and sprinkle each slice with the Parmesan cheese.

Place several mushrooms on each slice of toast and top with two asparagus spears. Salt and pepper to taste.

Serves 6

Polenta Rounds Topped with Goat Cheese

1 ½ cups water
1 ½ cups milk
1 cup yellow cornmeal
1 cup grated pecorino cheese
2 tablespoons olive oil
5 ounces soft goat cheese, brought to room temperature
½ cup thick tomato sauce
1/8 cup grated Parmesan cheese
Black pepper

Mix water and milk in saucepan. Bring to near boil. Pour cornmeal into the hot liquid in slow stream. Stir several minutes until the cornmeal reaches the consistency of hot cooked cereal. Stir in grated cheese. Grease an 8"x 8" baking dish with 1 tablespoon olive oil. Pour cooked polenta into the greased pan. Cool for 30 minutes.

Cut firm polenta into five 3" circles and remove from pan. Sauté polenta rounds in 1 tablespoon olive oil, a few minutes on each side.

Top each warmed polenta round with a layer of softened goat cheese.

Heat tomato sauce. Spoon a tablespoon of tomato sauce on top of the goat cheese. Sprinkle with Parmesan cheese and pepper.

Serves 5

Roasted Chicken with Rosemary Potatoes

1 chicken, cut into serving pieces
6 Idaho potatoes
¼ cup olive oil
Salt and pepper to taste
¼ cup rosemary leaves
2 finely chopped garlic cloves
¼ cup coarsely chopped parsley

Preheat oven to 375 degrees. Rinse chicken pieces and place them in roasting pan.

Peel the potatoes. Cut potatoes lengthwise into large wedges. Place the potatoes in the pan around the chicken.

Drizzle half of the olive oil over the chicken and potatoes. Sprinkle chicken and potatoes with salt and pepper, and one half the rosemary, garlic and parsley. Crush rosemary with fingers as you sprinkle it.

Turn the chicken and potatoes and drizzle with the remaining olive oil. Sprinkle chicken and the potatoes with salt, pepper, and remaining rosemary, chopped garlic and parsley.

Bake at 375 degrees for 1 1/4 hours, until the chicken reaches an internal temperature of 190 degrees and the potatoes are browned.

Serves 4

Biscotti

3/4 stick butter
3/4 cup sugar
1/4 cup oil
3 large eggs
1 teaspoon vanilla extract
1 teaspoon anise extract
3 cups flour
1 tablespoons baking powder
1/2 teaspoon salt
1 cup slivered almonds

Bring all ingredients to room temperature.   Preheat oven to 350 degrees.

Cream the butter and sugar with an electric mixer.

Add oil, eggs, vanilla and anise to mixture and beat until light and fluffy.

Combine flour, baking powder and salt. Add to batter and mix well. Mix in the almonds.

Using a light touch, roll the dough into a ball and cut into quarters. Roll each quarter into a 12 inch long stick.   Place the 4 sticks on a greased cookie sheet.

Bake at 350 degrees for 25 minutes.

Carefully remove the biscotti sticks to a cutting board. Slice at an angle into 3 inch long cookies.

Return the sliced cookies to the baking sheet cut side down. Bake for 10 minutes. Turn over the cookies and brown for 10 more minutes. Remove the biscotti and cool them on a wire rack.

Makes 3 dozen biscotti

Mailing List

To receive your notice of the next Karen Prince Mystery

Send your name and address to:

Galena Publishing

PO Box 18

Galena, IL 61036

Or email: skprincipe@aol.com. You can send your email address if you would prefer to be notified electronically.

You can use this page, or a copy of it:

Name:_____

Street
Address:_____

City, State and Zip code:_____

Email Address: _____

Additional Autographed Copies

of

Murder on the Mississippi

and **Murder in Galena**

ORDER FORM

Please send me:

_____ autographed copies of Murder on the Mississippi

_____ autographed copies of Murder in Galena

I enclose $15.50 for each copy. Please make check payable to: Galena Publishing.

Shipping Charges are $2.50 per book.

Please add 6.25% sales tax if shipped to an Illinois address.

Send my books to:

Name: _____

Street Address: _____

City and State: _____

Zip Code: _____

Mail this form to: **Galena Publishing**

PO Box 18

Galena, IL 61036

About the Author

Sandra Principe lives with her husband in the countryside near Galena. A Chicago lawyer for 20 years, she moved to the Galena area in 1996 to write and paint. She received her Bachelor of Science in English Education and her Juris Doctorate Degree from the University of Wisconsin, Madison.

Ms. Principe's paintings have been shown in galleries and museums across the country from Florida to California. This novel is a unique combination of her special knowledge of Galena, Kauai, painting and mysteries. Ms. Principe's first mystery, Murder in Galena, was published in 2003. This is the second in the Karen Prince Galena Mystery Series.

See Sandra Principe's paintings and learn more about her work at: **www.sandraprincipe.com**

www.ingramcontent.com/pod-product-compliance
Lightning Source LLC
Chambersburg PA
CBHW020332260626
47156CB00004B/1496